In the Absence of Spring

Alexander Graeme

Copyright © 2025 Alexander Graeme

All rights reserved.

ISBN: 9798309183821

Cover design by ZilverGlass

DEDICATION

To Spring.

CONTENTS

1. SUMMER   A Man of Paper and Ink   1
2. AUTUMN   A Soul of Ash   65
3. WINTER   A Dream of Bones   109

PART 1

SUMMER

A Man of Paper and Ink

CHAPTER ONE
The Unmade World

It may have been summer, but dampness defined the morning. It was the sort of damp that didn't cling, but seeped, as though the city itself endeavoured to weep through its stone pores. Hugo stood lingering at the edge of the curb, the cobblestones beneath his old shoes shining like scattered teeth that were glistening after a long night of rain. The sky hung heavy over the city, like a nascent thought already sinking. Hugo thought the world seemed unmade today, as if someone had forgotten to finish drawing it.

As he stood there, a young paperboy passed him, yelling out headlines with the conviction of someone who didn't understand a single word of them. "Progress!" the boy cried, brandishing papers above his head like a prophet heralding salvation. His voice cracked with each new syllable, "Cables across the ocean! The future has arrived!"

Hugo flinched at that last part. *The future,* he mused, a new century was here. It unfolded like a tempest—sudden and relentless, sweeping through without regard. It never sought consent, nor did it pause to ascertain if anyone was prepared for it. Hugo adjusted the collar of his coat, his fingers brushing against the threadbare wool. The fabric, much like himself, felt out of place, but the streets didn't care—they swallowed him anyway.

Just across the street, a woman in a red coat leaned against an off-angled lamppost, the cigarette between her fingers conjuring faint, curling phantoms. Her presence was sharp—too sharp for a morning like this. She ought to have blurred at the edges, but no, she stood there sharply defined, every movement deliberate. Hugo stared at her a moment too long, as if hoping she'd look back at him and notice the distaste on his face—but she did not. He envied her. No, that wasn't quite accurate. He loathed her—or, at least, he hated the ease with which she occupied space. She was someone who could laugh—resoundingly, without reservation—and not one person would think her foolish for it. Deep down, Hugo feared she was more real than he was.

It was then that the violin started. A prolonged, trembling note spilled over from above, weaving through the air with greater finesse than the lady in red's cigarette smoke. Hugo tilted his head, searching for the source, but the music eluded him, folding itself into the sounds of carts and footsteps all around him. The beauty, unlike Hugo's usual perception of violins, lacked innate sorrow; it overflowed with something inexpressible. Perhaps it was anticipation—the kind that made the air feel fuzzy.

By the time he looked back, the woman in red was gone, and he thought the street seemed emptier in her absence. Hugo lingered a moment longer, hands deep in his pockets, and his shoulders rounded under the weight of the morning. Just a few paces down the road, a bakery's shutters creaked open, spilling out some warmth and the faint scent of bread into the street. Hugo inhaled, ravenously filling his lungs with the smell. Then, a boy with smudged cheeks darted past, carrying a basket of rolls too big for his thin arms. He didn't look at Hugo, and Hugo didn't expect him to.

The city moved around him, as it always did—London seldom stopped for anything—its rhythm both constant and indifferent. Steam rose from grates, a man yelled at his horse, and somewhere in the distance, a church bell tolled. The unwavering bustle of the streets swallowed everything almost immediately.

Finally, Hugo began walking, his steps predictably uneven on the slick stones. The office waited for him—as it always did—patient and cold. Each day he returned to it like a penitent, though what sin he was atoning for, he could not say. The thought almost made him smile. Almost.

He passed by a flower cart; its vibrant blossoms were a stark contrast to the city's drab backdrop. A burly woman with wind-roughened cheeks called out to him. "Rose for the gentleman?" A harsh, unfamiliar accent coloured her question as she presented a single stem, like some priceless gem. Hugo shook his head, trying not to make eye contact, but the woman persisted. "For a lady, then?"

"There is no lady," he mumbled, almost apologetically, unsure she even heard him. The vendor frowned and turned her attention to another passerby. Hugo just kept on walking, his hands tightening in his pockets.

When he reached the office, the door creaked in protest as he pushed it open. The familiar scent of ink and damp paper greeted him bittersweet, while the indistinct murmur of voices made him yearn for just one day of silence. Rows of identical desks stretched out before him, their occupants hunched over their work, reminiscent of monks labouring in a scriptorium.

Hugo's desk was near a window, though the offered view was less than inspiring—just the sight of another nondescript building. He shed his coat and hung it on the back of his chair before sitting down to stare at a blank page.

The dense, precise papers of German text he was about to translate lay neatly to one side. He picked up the first sheet and ran his eyes along the first line, his pen hovering above the empty page below. Almost immediately, his mind wandered, the words dissolving into meaningless shapes.

His gaze drifted to the window, ignoring the uninspiring view, instead focusing on a spot of glass where a single drop of water traced a languorous path downward. Outside, the city continued its ceaseless, unforgiving motion, oblivious to the stillness within the office walls.

Hugo sighed and set his pen down. He leaned back in his chair and closed his eyes. The faint strains of a violin found their way into his memory, and he wondered who had been playing. What kind of person woke up on a damp summer morning and chose to fill the air with such sounds?

He thought about leaving. Just standing up, walking out the door, and pursuing the music, the flower cart, or the woman in red, wherever they might have gone. The thought was foolish, of course, and Hugo was well aware of that. That was his problem. He was always too aware.

Instead, he straightened in his chair and reached for his pen again. "What am I doing here?" he whispered to himself. The question hung in the air, without an answer, as he dipped the pen into the ink and began to write.

CHAPER TWO
A Violinist's Call

Lunch arrived unexpectedly. Though Hugo regarded his work as an exercise in tedium, he would often find himself entering a trance-like state when he got going. That trance carried him forward in time, releasing him only when he'd conquered a significant span of existence. Hugo had his own philosophical qualms with the concept of time, but those grievances were far too intricate to unravel while his stomach incessantly growled at him.

Hugo experienced a marginal improvement in mood upon reaching the city's open air. He had long concluded London's air paled in comparison to Berlin's, but it remained a welcome break from his monotonous office.

Far from being a socialite, Hugo almost never conversed with any of his fellow workmates. Aside from the occasional morning pleasantries—which he despised because of their superficiality—Hugo kept entirely to himself.

Recalling the heartwarming aroma he had encountered during his morning walk, Hugo acutely yearned for the warmth of freshly baked bread, and so he allowed his feet to lead him towards the bakery. As he navigated the streets of London once more—now throbbing with the vibrant rhythm of midday—Hugo struggled to fully liberate himself from the haze that had sailed with him through the morning.

Afternoons were always the nadir of his vitality. A morning person, Hugo was not, but at least they offered him a fresh canvas—an opportunity for renewal that he did not relish, but which nonetheless ignited the faintest flicker of stimulation. Hugo's bitterness was most pronounced in the hours after waking, easily provoked by the slightest irritation.

The evenings, as they descended into night's depths, were what Hugo cherished most dearly. It was in those hours, when the city surrendered itself to slumber, that Hugo's mind truly came alive. Sleep was a foreign concept to him, one he often scrutinised, but never regretted missing. While the world slept, a fierce lucidity ignited Hugo, inundating him with a torrent of ideas cascading from unknown cosmic sources. He drowned almost every night, and he would not have had it any other way.

Conversely, he found afternoons uninspiring. After emerging from the ritualistic constraints of the morning, then being subjected to hours of unrewarding labour squandered his potential, Hugo then had to endure the bustle of midday crowds, utterly devoid of enthusiasm while he did so. But this day bore a different cadence.

Before he could reach the bakery, a familiar melody drifted to his ears, stopping him in his tracks. In an instant, it was as though he had just surfaced from a deep, dreamless sleep. He instinctively stood taller, somehow awakened by the plaintive strains of the violinist from that morning. The long, drawn-out notes languished in the air, almost like they were sulking in his ears. He yearned to surrender to their call, and just like that, his appetite for bread waned, replaced by another, much different singular desire.

The music drew him to a nearby garden—an expanse teeming with greenery, suffused with the golden glow of the afternoon sun. He hadn't realised it, but the city had dried up since he had got to the office. He could scarcely believe this bright green landscape was within the same borders as the depressing surroundings that had dulled his senses. The elusive violinist remained hidden from his view, but the resounding notes told him they were near—perhaps just beyond the dense bushes ahead, just past the solitary woman seated on the bench.

That bench. Dressed in vibrant red, sat the same woman from that morning, the one who had stirred feelings of disdain in him. The one who smoked incessantly, indifferent to the world around her. The one who dared make him grapple with the question of whether she was more real than he was.

Hugo could no longer make out the violin, though its dazzling melodies were undoubtedly still occupying the surrounding space.

With hesitant steps, he etched his way towards her, trying not to seem too conspicuous. His eyes traced her shape, taking in every detail of her appearance. She possessed an air of muted focus, her enormous eyes fixed diligently on her sketchbook as her pencil danced quickly but methodically over the page. Her wavy golden-brown hair fluttered gently against her hunched-over shoulders as the summer breeze passed over her. No, this wasn't her—this was someone else entirely, someone less real.

Unable to contain himself, Hugo exhaled a sigh that startled the woman, who seemed to have been so enveloped in her artistry that she hadn't even realised he had been standing so close to her. The sudden noise led to her sketchbook thudding against the stone beneath the bench, and Hugo, feeling an awkward wave of remorse, wasted no time in crouching down to fetch it for her. When he stood, holding the book in his hands, he cast a swift glance at its contents, discovering a rough, but skilful sketch of the city skyline—though it was not all it appeared to be at first glance. The drawing exhibited a surrealness, with exaggerated shapes and angles that clamoured for his attention.

Abruptly aware that he had lingered over the artwork for too long, Hugo awkwardly handed the sketchbook back to her without uttering a word. The slight nod of his head was so discreet, thus unclear if she had even caught it.

"Thank you," the woman said with a smile, but he avoided meeting her eye. He seemed content to just dwell in the uncomfortable silence that had manifested between them.

"It doesn't take courage to be kind, you know," she remarked with what seemed to be a gentle challenge.

"Courage?" Hugo's cheeks flushed with embarrassment, and his accent thickened as he stumbled over his words. "I wouldn't presume that giving a lady… no… pick… I wouldn't think to claim that picking up a lady's drawings signifies bravery."

"Not for the sketchbook, for the eye contact."

Hugo's face turned an even deeper shade of red, and for a split second, he dared to meet her gaze. It was fleeting—so brief in its essence that it barely constituted a genuine encounter—but it revealed an unsettling truth: he had been mistaken about her in a way he had never been mistaken about anyone before. Yes, she was less real than he was, that much he had correctly ascertained, but he had fallen short of the full realisation. This woman was so ethereal that she had emerged as the most genuinely real entity he had ever encountered. The swirling cobalt depths of her eyes harboured the entirety of the cosmos, encompassing all its mysteries—both real and fantastical.

"I must beg my leave," he muttered before scurrying off like the rodent he had just metamorphosed into under the weight of her scrutiny.

To be perceived was seldom desirable and was always the end of the world.

CHAPTER THREE
The City Dreams

The next morning, Hugo woke up an hour earlier than he usually did. An unusual fervour fuelled him, pulsating through his body like a slumbering flame re-ignited. Hugo felt lasting excitement; a first for what seemed ages. When he had returned to the office following his lunch break the day prior, it was the first time he had ever fallen behind on his work. Unlike the usual trance that guided him, thoughts of the woman from the garden instead consumed his mind. Its continuation marked his journey home and subsequent evening. It struck him that he was a fool—he hadn't even considered asking her name.

Lunch could not come fast enough. When it finally did, he rushed from the office, eliciting bemused glances from his colleagues, who likely regarded his sudden eagerness with a mix of confusion and indifference. But the fleeting interest of his coworkers dissipated as readily as smoke, for Hugo was not a man who inspired their contemplation.

Hugo was as antisocial as they came, never displaying interest in anything outside of his work. He was an outsider, a German navigating life in London, and the singular representation of his nationality within the office. Complicated perceptions of Germany existed among the British. Admiration coexisted with anxiety surrounding Germany's growing industrial prowess, colonial ambitions, and military might. The German demographic in London had burgeoned of late, diversifying its presence across various social strata in both the East and West Ends.

Hugo had made no effort to integrate into the social fabric of his workplace, but on the rare occasion when someone dared to initiate conversation, his accent immediately tethered him to an identity of otherness before he could even express himself—a constant reminder that he would never quite belong. It was a testament to his life story—always an outsider, misunderstood by everyone. His distant and awkward manner only deepened the divide between him and his peers, with others usually mistaking his introspection for arrogance and his discomfort for disdain. Not that he didn't feel those ways too—he often did.

There was no violin to guide him that afternoon, but that did not matter—Hugo knew exactly where he needed to take himself. He hastened towards the same garden he'd been led to the day before, forgoing another overdue visit to the bakery. Similar to before, afternoon warmth and brightness evoked an almost heavenly cheer. The gorgeous spot of green stood out as a paradise amongst the city, though in truth to Hugo, that was primarily down to the enchanting English rose he found blooming there.

Hugo slowed, hesitation gnawing at his resolve as he approached the bench. There she was, lost in her sketches, just like the day before. Today, she wore violet instead of red, and she had braided her hair, framing her delicate features. But for Hugo, there was no mistaking her, for although he did not understand it, the impression she had made on him was there to stay, akin to a livestock brandishing being seared mercilessly into his helpless obstinate brain.

"Miss..." he coughed and cleared his throat. "Do you mind?"

"I thought you might be back," she said as she smiled up at him. Those enormous eyes—disproportionate for her face—harboured a depth of complexity that overwhelmed him, to a greater extent than he had first perceived. She shifted herself on the bench, ensuring her frock was not in the way as the peculiar German man took a seat beside her.

The young woman continued sketching while Hugo sat beside

her in contemplative silence, anxiously scratching at the already irritated skin on the back of his hand. Side-eyeing her, he observed her awkward posture—bewildered by how it belonged to the same woman who housed infinity in her eyes. An insatiable curiosity grew within him as he made a discreet attempt to observe her drawing.

"Here," she said, her soft voice slicing through the silence, and his face turned scarlet. How had she noticed him looking? She had kept her eyes fixed on the paper. Hugo reluctantly accepted that his attempts at discretion had been woefully ineffective. As she relinquished the sketchbook to him, he took a mental note of her perfect, slender fingers.

Hugo inspected the drawing for some time. At first, it appeared to be the same one from the day before—a skilful sketch of London's skyline, bearing certain uncanny, exaggerated features. But something was off. A subtle different caught Hugo's eye, one that was slight, but profound enough to suggest that this drawing was distinct from the previous one. "These lines," he eventually spoke, "they are not like before. They are thicker, bolder—yet less certain of themselves."

She quickly snatched the book back from him. Now it was she who had some pink in her cheeks. "You see things most people miss, don't you?"

"I see... too much. Sometimes. It is not always a blessing."

She turned her head and looked straight into his eyes. "Maybe it's not supposed to be. Look here," she directed his attention back to the paper as she flicked back a page. "This was from yesterday, and this is from today. I was shocked that you noticed such a subtle difference after only a brief look at yesterday's. The difference in thickness is so little."

"To me, it is blinding," he said. "But what purpose does this serve? How is it that yesterday's lines possess a confidence that today's lack, despite being less pronounced? Surely, you have some intended meaning, do you not?"

"Must there always be meaning in the things a woman does?"

"Oh, most definitely," Hugo declared, a fervent passion bursting through his eyes. "Every act in this life carries meaning, even those that profess to be devoid of it. Your every breath resonates with significance; when you spread jam upon your morning bread, you may believe you are merely satiating your early-day appetite, but consciously or not, it transcends that simplicity. Consider for a moment the incredible journey that took place across so many lives, just for you to savour that one moment. Think of all the individuals involved nurturing and harvesting the crops and fruits. Reflect on the labour needed to transform those elements into the bread and jam that later came to be on your breakfast table. Consider the intricacies of packaging, of transport, and of the sale. All of these parts link countless souls to something as seemingly mundane as your breakfast habits. And well, you may be inclined to dismiss this all as a byproduct of the world we live in, but I reject that notion entirely. Each soul is dancing with the universe, for each is the universe. You, in a convoluted, roundabout way, have partaken in the entire process. That is the meaning. Thus, every line you etch into that paper undoubtedly has meaning. The correct question here is not whether your drawing carries meaning, but whether it bears an intended one. You must excuse my forwardness, but I do not believe you to be a woman who lacks intention."

"You never introduced yourself," she said with a wide smile across her face.

"I am Hugo," he said, reaching clumsily for her hand to gently plant a kiss.

"It's a pleasure to make your acquaintance, Hugo," she replied, a soft giggle escaping her lips at his awkwardness. "I am Emily."

"How do you do, Emily?"

"I think the time for pleasantries has elapsed, Hugo. Wouldn't you agree?"

"Indeed. I have never been fond of such talk."

"Then it appears we share a sentiment," she said, observing as Hugo straightened with newfound attentiveness. There was something infectious about her energy, so much so that Hugo was now brandishing his first genuine smile in weeks. "People say this city never sleeps… I believe it dreams. The kind you wake up from unsure of who you really are."

"If it dreams, then I suppose I am the nightmare."

"You?" Emily chortled. "You're not nearly dramatic enough for that." Her laughter felt akin to sunlight breaking through a canopy of clouds; it was momentary, but impossible for him to forget.

"You jest, but only because you have yet to see the anguished beast that is my spirit."

"That was sarcasm, Hugo," she clarified, her fingers gently grazing his arm—a touch that made his insides burn and scream, as though she had been a priest performing an exorcism. "As I was saying, I believe the city dreams. I believe that with all my heart. Look again, here, these lines from today are thicker, yes, that's because they represent that sort of thick hazy feeling you get when you wake up and try to remember an elusive dream. That's why, despite them being bolder, they are less certain. So many of us go about our lives, wholly ignorant of our true selves. We may think we know ourselves, but we don't. And that's why when we look back here at yesterday's sketch, the lines are more delicate, yet more confident. They symbolise the ego of man—he who believes himself to be acquainted with his own nature but remains profoundly unaware."

"And the exaggerated angles," Hugo eagerly jumped in, "they exemplify the delusion? A surreal quality manifests here because none of it ever existed in truth, even when the most earnest believers are convinced otherwise."

"Exactly. Tell me, Hugo, how is it you can so quickly switch from brooding contemplation to optimistic ruminations on the nature of the universe, only to retreat once again into brooding?"

"You presume much, Emily. My beliefs regarding the universe are neither positive nor negative, they simply… are. Optimism is the least of my concerns. In fact, I would go as far as to say I often exhibit signs of an aversion to its persistent presence. But let us return to the topic of your drawings; I must make it known to you that I admire them greatly."

His words seemed to fill her with joy, prompting her to peruse further pages of her sketchbook. "I have many more…" she faltered, her gaze lifting to meet his with uncharacteristic shyness. "If you'd like to see them."

"Of course!" he exclaimed. "Show me everything." They spent a long time looking over the subsequent drawings together. Most were landscapes; others were portraits, yet each shared a subtle degree of surrealism. All of Emily's drawings contained some element that distanced her work from mundane reality. Emily occasionally exaggerated shapes and angles, distorting subjects' faces and bending landscapes; at other times, she entirely replaced expectations with unforeseen elements. In one scene, she uprooted a solitary tree, substituting it with an exceptionally tall pencil.

"Your talent is immense."

"Each time I finish a piece, I can't help but feel sad," she confessed, "for it is my dream to make a living as an artist, but it appears the world desires only to mock my ambition. I am told that I squander myself; that I hurt my family by not yet having children. And now, as I approach my twenty-eighth birthday, I look back on the past decade of my artistic endeavours, and all I feel is shame. Yet I cannot relinquish my passion. While I have given up on my paintings, another obsession has filled the space left behind. Now, I spend my afternoons here, in this garden, alone, sketching skylines while consumed by future anxieties. I fear I will become bitter like my mother—oh, she is such a hard woman."

"Forgive my prying, but do you—"

"I live alone, away from my family, subsisting on a stipend given in secret by my elder sister. Francis was fortunate to find herself as the cherished darling to The Earl of Plymouth, who wasted little time before putting a ring around her finger."

She hadn't exactly said it, but Hugo knew. Emily was like him—she understood. They both felt the same way about their parents, and oh, how Hugo felt it in his bones when she spoke of her obsessions, of how she discarded one only to have it supplanted by another.

"What have you done to me, Hugo?"

"Huh? I know not what you imply, I don't think I—"

"Relax," she reassured him, her hand brushing against his arm again. "I simply mean… how have you brought me to this?"

"I don't understand. To what?"

"To the surface. For the first time in a long time, I feel as though I can breathe. You know, I have come here to this garden every day this summer—in fact, I began midway through spring. In all that time, I have not engaged in a substantive conversation with even one person, until today."

"From my perspective, it is you who has dragged me from the depths, dear Emily, not the other way around. I scarcely recall having spoken to anyone as intently since, well, perhaps since my arrival here. I seldom make it past social pleasantries, and I usually avoid those."

For the first time since the conversation began, there was a brief silence. Not because they had nothing more to say—that couldn't have been further from the truth—but because they each had finally found some solace within this tumultuous landscape of lukewarm dreams.

"Do you ever feel like you are waiting for something?" Emily asked, breaking the silence. "As though the world owes you a moment that hasn't yet arrived?"

"I do not think of myself as a man who likes to wait. I am unconvinced that time even exists, yet it feels like a thread wound far too tight. It continues to fray at the edges, and I swear I can hear it snapping, one fibre at a time. I believe the world has already spent whatever it owed me, dear Emily. I'm just trying to make sense of the leftovers."

"What do you expect to find when that final fibre snaps?"

"Meaning."

"I thought you already had meaning? You asserted that everything does."

"I said that everything holds meaning, yes. I did not claim that we are privy to the form that meaning takes—that is a different matter entirely."

A moment of reprieve followed.

"You're not from here…"

"What gave it away?" Hugo joked with a smile. "Was it my soothing personality?" It might have been his first joke since arriving in London.

"Actually, it was the ring."

"British men wear rings."

"They do, but not ones embellished with German insignia. I believe they typically reserve such adornments for men of German descent."

Hugo glanced to the side and fiddled with the ring around his finger. Although he rarely thought about it, the ring represented his last connection to his heritage; his great-grandfather had passed it down, and he had secretly taken it from his father before leaving Berlin. It brought him no joy to wear, and yet he could not bring himself to part with it for any reason.

"What brought you to London, Hugo?"

Hugo held back a great sigh. "The short answer… hope."

"What was it you hoped for?"

"Perhaps I phrased that wrongly. A more accurate answer would be… a profound absence of hope. There was no hope for me in Germany. It is true that my country is gaining strength now—our people are building for the future—but there is nothing there for me. My family and I always had a tempestuous relationship, but roughly three years ago, we said things to each other that could never be taken back. You mentioned your mother, and I must confess that mine is not so different, but for me, the more formidable obstacle is my father. Our philosophical discord runs deep. For him, it is unacceptable for anyone within our lineage to oppose his directives. Our family possessed wealth, so I gathered what I needed, and I left. I arrived in London in March of 1897, twenty-seven years old, with no children, and never married. I spent a long time striving for meaningful employment where I might apply my education, but in my haste to flee Berlin, I neglected essential documents and credentials. Of course, my family is not likely to facilitate their retrieval. So now I am trapped in the best position I attain without my documents. Day after day, I translate a plethora of German papers into English. I fear I may have left one hopeless place only to ensnare myself in another."

His words, though passionate, were dramatic. While he may have relinquished all hope in Berlin, a flicker of aspiration yet danced within him here in London. He had yet to exhaust all his potential avenues, and a newfound connection with Emily had summoned a blaze within his soul. Even so, Hugo's hope felt fragile—like cradling a moth in his palms, terrified that it might disintegrate or fly away.

"I am so sorry to hear all of that, Hugo. Accounts of tragic families distress me. But I have faith in you. You'll find your purpose."

"Oh!" Hugo sprang to his feet, startling Emily in the process.

"What's the matter?" she asked.

"I've been gone too long. This was to be just a quick lunch break. I must get back."

"Will you return tomorrow?" she inquired, standing beside him, her gaze reaching his jawline.

"What time?"

She smiled for a moment before answering. "I thought you said time didn't exist?"

"And yet, I am forced to live within its constraints."

CHAPTER FOUR
Prison of Ice

That night, Hugo tossed and turned for hours, unable to elude the lingering echoes of his earlier conversation with Emily. He found himself obsessively replaying every word exchanged between them. There was so much he regretted not articulating, so much he longed to have expressed, and an even greater expanse of inquiries left unvoiced. The knowledge that he would encounter her again the following day offered little in the way of comfort; rather, it only exacerbated the relentless churn of thoughts within him, urgently probing every conceivable avenue of dialogue yet to be traversed.

It was just after three when Hugo decided to give up on the futile attempt to quiet his mind. Fortunately, he had a tried and tested solution for such occasions—one he relied upon with alarming frequency. While effective in lulling him into sleep, this solution came at a disheartening cost to his liver. A half-bottle of brandy later, he found himself fortunate that his neighbours did not choose to lodge a complaint regarding the sounds of a wild animal nesting above them.

He dreamt of the sun, its radiant warmth promising to thaw the frigid prison encasing him. Alone in a block of ice, in the centre of Berlin, the people of the world disregarded him as they went about their lives. Immobility ensnared him, forcing him to watch familiar and unfamiliar faces pass without a glance. The city was alive, and it did not need him. Worse yet, it did not want him.

An eternity unfurled, yet his plight remained unchanged. His surroundings were dry; the sun was in the sky. But his predicament persisted. He grew convinced that the sun itself was a liar and soon found himself consumed by burning desire—a conflagration of rage, the urge to scream invectives at the sky, to scold its resident luminary for all of its untruths. *You are supposed to represent hope,* he inwardly seethed. *Instead, you are nought but a cruel façade. You have soiled my soul, and you have doomed us all.*

But perhaps he had reached his damning conclusion too soon, for instantaneously after his lamentation, warmth began to touch him… and the ice began to melt.

Hugo woke up panting, his pillowcase soaked right through. He could not decide whether to label it a night terror, or just an ordinary dream. It had only been forty minutes since he last remembered glancing at the clock. He reached for the glass perched on the nightstand, gulping down the dregs of brandy that still resided at the bottom. After setting the glass back down, he turned the pillow over, rolled onto his side, and fought his way back to sleep.

CHAPTER FIVE
The Tragedy of the Ordinary

The music had returned. Despite his mapped-out intentions, when the morrow dawned, and he approached the bench to greet the alluring Emily, Hugo found himself distracted—captured by the lilting strains of the nearby violin. The German had meticulously planned every aspect of their encounter, beginning with a compliment regarding her enchanting eyes, followed by a daring kiss on the soft skin of her hand. But, as if bewitched, the music that seemed to re-tune his mental frequency had disrupted his plans. By the time he found himself in front of dear Emily, the words he had so carefully prepared had slipped from his grasp, stolen from him by the enchantment of the melody.

"Good afternoon, Hugo," she spoke first—rising to her feet—thus disrupting the plans he had failed to enact. His brain in shambles, he searched for the right words while he reached out for her hand, only to find that Emily had no desire for such an overture. Instead, she sprang onto her toes, planting the most delicate of kisses upon his cheek before retreating to her perch on the bench. The action left Hugo flustered and speechless.

"Will you sit with me?" she asked with rosy cheeks, and of course, he did.

"I've never understood why people say that."

"Good afternoon?"

"Yes… well, the 'good' part… or the 'afternoon' part… both, I suppose." Hugo scratched behind his ear with an earnestness that rendered him almost animalistic in his awkwardness.

"Are you alright? You seem... odd. Not to say your past eccentricities were unwelcome, but your eccentricity today is of a different sort. In fact, I think it resembles the type of oddness you exhibited on the day you first came here—the day you picked up my sketchbook."

"Forgive my disarray," Hugo pleaded. "It's the music—it does something to me. That was, in fact, my motivation for coming here that first time, but then you distracted me."

"You would ascribe blame to a wholly unremarkable woman for your own lack of self-discipline?" Emily feigned indignation, her eyes sparkling with mischief.

"Not at all!" Hugo protested. "I would never blame—"

"So, you agree I am unremarkable?" she teased.

"Oh, dear Emily, there has never been a greater mistruth uttered on this earth."

"Do you intend to part with that rose, or is it an accessory?"

Hugo considered himself a fool. The afternoon had not at all gone how he had intended—the plans that had danced in his mind could not have been more different. It had started when he struggled to find the florist's cart, which was usually always in the same spot. He had sweat stains under his arms to show for his mad rush around the streets in search of it.

"For you, dear Emily," he reached out to hand her the single lavender rose he had procured.

"Everything has meaning," she said, recalling his words from the day before. "Thank you, Hugo. This is gorgeous."

Hugo should have been pleased with himself—it was clear that Emily genuinely appreciated the rose he gave her—yet he remained distant.

"You are here every day, Emily... do you know the musician who plays so beautifully?"

"Sorry, Hugo, but I do not."

"At least let me know if they are a man or a woman."

"I'm afraid I cannot. Truly, I have not cast my eyes upon them even once. The first time I heard the sounds of the violin was the same day you first came to the garden."

"How peculiar..." he turned his head slowly, looking off into the distance as if following a phantom trail of musical notes through the air with his eyes.

"Should we investigate?" Emily touched his wrist.

Hugo seemed conflicted by her suggestion. "No," he eventually said, "I believe it better left a mystery. This way, it could be anyone playing."

"Will it not bother you to remain oblivious to the truth? Will you not lie awake at night, tormented by the thoughts of the violinist's identity?"

Her words seemed to amuse Hugo, who allowed a broad smile to take hold of his expression. "I assure you, my nocturnal habits will remain unchanged. Furthermore, imagine if we ventured forth, rounded the corner, and discovered an utterly ordinary individual. Would that not constitute a tragedy? A devastating blow to the fantasy."

"You speak of ordinary as if it were some disease. I find no harm in the idea of the violinist being a commonplace person. What would you prefer instead? A deranged soul or an armless woman? Perhaps a grand elephant pouring its heart into the performance?"

"Oh, but my dear Emily, ordinariness is precisely that—a lamentable state. I say this: to be ordinary is to suffer a grave illness surpassing all others. I spend all of my days striving to avoid those who are ordinary, and I have always found myself infinitely more at ease in the company of even the most grotesque, repulsive individuals than with the most inoffensive of normal folk. Please, do not mistake my sentiments for an appraisal of loathsome creatures; such beings are, undoubtedly, detestable. What is clear to me, however, is that the ordinary man is far more insidious to society at large. At first glance, he appears harmless, but as an artist, you surely recognise the depths of deception that surface appearances can veil. For you see, dear Emily, the ordinary man may move through the world, seeking not to bother anyone else, and in return, not to be bothered himself, but this inevitably leads him down a path of uncontested apathy. Before long, he finds himself as part of the herd—a herd shepherded by powers that serve the interests of the few. This herd instinctively rejects the nonconformist and pressures our most brilliant minds to suppress their authentic selves for fear of ridicule or reprisal. Thus, while the ordinary man may not directly inflict harm, he continuously and unapologetically stifles the spirit of the world around him, albeit indirectly. To return to the idea of the abhorrent, but strange individual: although I may abhor them and their moral failings, I will always carry a begrudging respect for the individuality they have so boldly brought to the table."

They sat for a long time, the violin still playing, while Emily processed everything Hugo had just thrown at her. It was as though he could not regulate himself, always oscillating between two extremes; either he was invisible—a man withdrawn so far into himself that the world had no clue he even existed—or he was a blinding light, a presence that unrelentingly seared his words and ideas into whoever he deemed worthy of hearing them. Hugo felt Emily's presence as if she opened the door to a troubled house he'd been locked inside for years—she was far beyond worthy.

"It stopped," Emily observed.

"Indeed. I'm afraid I must be getting back." Hugo, though not one to show grand expressions on his face often, looked somewhat sad.

"You've scarcely arrived!"

"Time does not exist, remember?"

"I did not even have the opportunity to respond to your diatribe on commonality. How is that fair?"

"Fairness is a concept of little consequence. I believe you travelled someplace else for a while, somewhere far warmer than London, where animals could sing, and churches could talk. You looked happy there; I could see the joy on your face. Were I even a fraction of the artist I understand you to be, I would seize that sketchbook and etch your image into permanence. Such beauty deserves to be captured—if not for eternity, then at least for as long as this infatuated man deigns to live. It seems you thought yourself absent for but a moment, but the truth is you vanished for a lifetime, and so now I must depart."

"I shall see you again, will I not?" she rose to her feet after him.

"Tomorrow. You are always here in the afternoon."

"No. This evening."

"This evening?"

"When you finish your work… return to me. I shall wait right here."

"Dear Emily, I will be labouring for a long while. For the first time in my life, I have fallen behind in my work. Today, I must stay longer to right the balance."

"Stop trying to dissuade me, you obstinate German. I care not how long it takes. I will be waiting here for you."

"I'm the stubborn one?"

"It is painfully evident."

"Very well, dear Emily, return to that place of wonder you visited before. I shall be back before you know it."

CHAPTER SIX
A Liar, Too

The rest of his workday was yet again suboptimal. Hugo had always been one of the most focused and efficient workers in the office. When he got into the zone, he thrived, accomplishing tasks with remarkable swiftness. It had always bothered him how his efficiency was never something that was rewarded, and the same was true throughout his whole life.

Whether it be in school, at home, or now in his work translating documents into English, Hugo had learned that speed in execution bore no reward. His rapid task completion consistently earned him only unenthusiastic praise, followed by extra assignments. It angered him that in response to his diligence, he was inundated with even more work. This had always been the pattern—Hugo labouring at the pace of three individuals while his colleagues stumbled through the meagre workload of one.

To top it all off, Hugo's high output only made things more difficult for himself. Taking his work as an example: at first, his superiors—who, as far as he was concerned, were superior in name only—would lavish him with praise, offering kind words about how his efficiency was a great asset to the company. But before long, that very efficiency ceased to elicit gratitude; it became an expectation rather than a compliment. Had it not been for this ungrateful acceptance of his capabilities, he doubted he would have fallen behind in the wake of his encounter with Emily in that enchanting garden. He managed to keep up with the basic workflow demanded of his peers, but he had spent so long doing more than twice what most others did, and so now the additional documents were beginning to accumulate on his desk.

As much as it bothered him that he received no benefits from working more efficiently than everyone else, it had never stopped him from continuing to do so. Tasks easily bore Hugo if he deemed them mundane or simple, and so the extra work helped keep him a tad more stimulated. His counterparts may have been more than happy to indulge in easy-going chatter to navigate the dullness of their days, but Hugo despised such frivolity. He would sooner drown himself in the frigid waters of the Thames than be seen engaging in trivial chit-chat with the ordinary man.

Hugo knew well that his own actions had forged his present predicament, but he couldn't imagine living any other way. When he entered his trance-like state of focus, there was just no stopping him—it was like someone else took over for him.

As the day waned and he departed the office, he had slashed the pile of documents on his desk, but it still wasn't enough. He understood that if he failed to regain his usual state of mind soon, then trouble would find him. That's what he got for spoiling his 'superiors' for so long.

When he finally arrived back at the garden to meet Emily, it was strangely quiet. Though the garden was typically quiet compared to other areas Hugo visited in the city, there was not a single person in sight that evening. Hugo struggled to remember the last time he had been alone somewhere outdoors in the city. But of course, he was not alone, for awaiting his return, still sitting on the bench as though she had never moved, was the young woman he was so transfixed by. When he saw her, her presence paralysed him for a moment. Engrossed in her sketching, she radiated a light that transcended the dimming sun. Despite some of their shared qualities, Hugo perceived her as something supernatural. Though she would have disagreed, to him she was the embodiment of dreams themselves, and as he had previously remarked to her, he saw himself as a nightmare incarnate. Yet even though he saw her so differently from himself in that regard, he deeply related to her, feeling drawn to her spirit ever since they first locked eyes. He understood its irrationality, admitting his foolishness, yet an obsession simmered—resisting control, defying dismissal.

"Your latest masterpiece?" Hugo spoke as he neared the bench.

"Oh," Emily seemed startled, flipping over her sketchbook to prevent him from catching sight of her work. "I hadn't noticed you'd arrived."

"I just got here. May I?"

"Yes, yes, of course," she invited him to sit with her. She seemed rather giddy, shuffling around on the bench while she fiddled with her hair, a marked contrast to their earlier encounter.

"So… your drawing…"

"Yes…"

"May I… see it?"

"Oh, heavens, no! It's not done. No, don't look at me like that. I will not reveal what isn't ready.

"Look at you like what?"

"Like a lost puppy. Hugo, I am fond of you, but you mustn't employ such tactics."

"I beg your pardon, dear Emily, but I must confess I am utterly baffled by your assertions. I am simply expressing a genuine admiration for your wondrous talent."

"Very well."

"When do you think it will be ready?"

"Soon, I hope. When it is, I will let you see it. I promise."

The pair sat without speaking a word for some time, though Hugo found himself desperate to voice a question that poised itself on the tip of his tongue. He could sense something in the air, something that was not quite right. When he looked at Emily, he observed how her body language had grown closed off, and her expression appeared far more rigid. Briefly, he wondered if she was feeling cold now that the sun was beginning its descent. Then he considered the length of time she had spent waiting for him to return. Yes, he had warned her he would be gone a long time, but Hugo had had experiences like this before.

Back in Berlin, in his early twenties, he had had a fleeting romance with a woman six years his senior, named Mathilda. At first, Hugo thought of Mathilda as a mature and understanding woman, and despite his parent's disapproval of her lowly station in life, he continued to see her. However, this illusion soon crumbled. With time, Mathilda's critical flaw became agonisingly apparent. She would endorse his thoughts and actions in the moment, only to later berate him for those very sentiments she had previously lauded.

For a second, Hugo allowed his mind to drift towards the unsettling notion that Emily might be the same. Was Hugo cursed to connect with women burdened by this same defect forever?

Eventually, he mustered up the courage to pose his simple, yet loaded, question. "Is something the matter?"

"I'm… not sure. I suppose part of me is trying to make sense of all this."

"Of what?"

"Me, this garden, life... you," she turned and met his gaze directly. Hugo sensed he'd crumble into dust, but he held on.

"Go on," he encouraged.

"You frequently bring up the concept of 'reality.' You suggest certain things possess a more profound importance than others do. Yet, Hugo, I wonder how I am to ascertain what is genuine. Time, nature, morality—how do I determine the authenticity of any of these? How am I to know if you even exist?"

Hugo was stunned. He had not expected such an answer from her.

"I come here each day, and I sketch. You say that everything holds meaning, and you gave an elaborate argument proposing that out interconnectedness implies inherent meaning; however, I must confess that I am unconvinced. More so, I fear you doubt many of your own assertions. You seem to champion—passionately—positions you do not honestly believe in. While I cannot definitively decide whether you grasp this disconnect, what I am sure of is that you have devoted an excessive amount of time to such contemplations of existence. I sense that. I know that. At first, when we met, I was in awe of your candour. But now, as I think back on our discussions, I have come to believe— not without some anguish—that you spend your days nestled in self-deception. That's not good, Hugo. And if you are lying to yourself, then that also means you are lying to me. If I am correct, which I believe I am, then I can I possibly trust that you are real at all?"

Hugo's eyes fell downward, for in that moment, he could no longer bear to look at her. If he did, he knew that he would die.

Emily took a deep breath and rubbed at her eyes before continuing. "But the worst part of all... is that I understand. I understand because I, too, am a liar. So, just as I cannot know if you exist, how is it you are supposed to know if I do?"

Hugo looked up at her, his eyes eventually coming upon her gentle face. Her smooth cheeks were damp with tears, and her bottom lip trembled. In that moment, all he wanted to do was reach out and embrace her, to hold her and tell her she mattered—that she existed more fervently than anyone he had ever known—but he could not, for that would have required Hugo Henke to exist, and Hugo Henke did not exist.

"Oh, I am so lonely, Hugo. It hurts so much. The ache is unbearable. I do not know how I am meant to bear this burden for the rest of my life. You understand how it feels, do you not? Don't you feel so alone?"

Hugo was not hasty in his reply, but his reply did come. "I am always lonely, but never alone. For my loneliness, dear Emily, is not a void, but a presence. It is a shadow that sits beside me at every meal and follows me down every street."

"That is so awful," Emily sniffed. "Beautiful... but awful."

"How is it that a thing as magnificent as you could end up so alone?"

A laugh escaped from beneath her tears, and a small bubble blew out her nose. Hugo fished out his handkerchief and extended it to her.

"You could have given me this earlier," she remarked. In truth, Hugo regretted offering her the handkerchief at all—not because he lacked the desire to help, but because of his firm belief that his earthly fabric was unworthy of her empyrean tears. He would never tell her that.

"Hugo..."

"Yes, dear Emily?"

"Will you walk me home? I'll tell you everything on the way."

CHAPTER SEVEN
A Heart Too Grand

As they strolled through the streets of London, Emily's woes spilled out into the space around them. The warmth of the day was slipping away, and the fading sunlight cast extended shadows that stretched like memories that stubbornly refused to let go.

Emily told Hugo of her childhood, of how she had grown up in a family that had been wealthy enough to shield her from hardship, but not from pain. Her father was a pragmatic, distant businessman, and he devoted himself to managing the family's finances and social standing, rarely sparing time for either of his daughters—far more captivated by the company of a bottle than familial ties. Burdened by the crushing weight of her own unfulfilled aspirations, Emily's mother unwound into a creature of bitterness, often wielding her sharp tongue like a weapon to control and wound those around her.

"Francis… she was everything they hoped for," Emily told him. "Charming, ambitious, and above all, she was dutiful—always adhering to the societal rules that governed our lives. My parents rejoiced when she married such an affluent man. She had consummated their dreams, solidifying her place as our family's crowning achievement, and my mother insisted everyone was to know her pride."

When Francis departed the family home to begin her life with her new husband, the departure left Emily behind in a home filled with echoes of her mother's disappointment. Worse yet, her father's indifference.

"My mother always loved to tell me how I'd never live up to

Francis. She'd often tell me I was born with too much heart and not enough spine. Those words stung deeply, as I have always believed that to have a grand heart is worth far greater merit than anything else. For what are we worth as human beings if we cannot extend kindness to one another? She would never have spoken such cutting words to Francis, even though she, too, lacked resolve. No, Francis never needed a spine—she had titles and rings to hold her up."

"She sounds cruel."

"I try not to think of her that way. She's just tired. Tired of me, tired of the life she chose, tired of pretending it's enough."

"Perhaps that is true, but regardless of what has happened in her life, nothing justifies the transference of her frustrations onto you."

"I know that, of course. In the end, it was one of the principal reasons I left home."

As they neared Emily's apartment, their pace slowed, as though she was intent on drawing out the conversation for as long as she could. "Loneliness defined my childhood," she said. "Though I suppose it may be more accurate to call it the theme of my life. My parents never endorsed my interests; they deemed my artistic inclinations frivolous at best, and a resounding failure to meet their expectations at worst. Francis's life wasn't easy—that's an unfair assessment—but unlike with me, others celebrated her. I was the quiet shadow, always on the periphery of my family's affection. My vivid memories include the evenings when my mother hosted extravagant dinners for my father's business associates or family friends. My absence always went unnoticed as I sat alone upstairs, listening to the murmur of voices from the party below. Sometimes, I wish I had had the audacity to peek into the room and say hello. My mother would have been furious, but at least then I'd have been able to make sure that they knew I was there."

"You left home," Hugo remarked. They had now come to a stop outside Emily's apartment. Externally, it lacked ostentation, yet it remained a desirable property—a stark contrast to Hugo's depressing dwelling. "That must have taken courage. You also speak your mind openly… even to a stranger such as I. From where I'm standing, you seem to have no shortage of bravery."

"That wasn't courage, it was survival. My mother made it abundantly clear just how much of a disappointment I was, and my father didn't even care enough to contest."

"But Francis—"

"Yes, Francis played her part perfectly. She married a man with a title, giving them everything they could have wanted, and now she pays for my freedom like it is charity."

"Can it be considered true freedom if you remain dependent on her?"

"I ask myself that every day. Naturally, she could never make it known to my parents that she supports me. My mother would more than decry such a revelation, and that's not a reality Francis is comfortable facing."

"Do they not wonder how you live as you do? Surely, they have their suspicions?"

"I am certain they do, but I remain oblivious to their musings. Although they still reside in London, I have not crossed paths with them since I left home. My departure made certain truths abundantly clear—they are not interested in my life."

"And Francis?"

"I resent her, though not through any fault of her own. Envy, I suppose. Though I do still love her dearly. Her living outside of London complicates things. I have visited her on a handful of occasions, just as she has occasionally sought me out when visiting our parents in the city. But there is no intimate sisterhood to speak of."

Hugo's heart sank for her—or was it for himself? Though her story was distinct from his in a myriad of ways, it resonated with him. Each revelation only boosted his admiration for her.

"It seems to me that the world is constantly moving without me. It's like everyone else has somewhere to be, someone to see, but I'm just… still. Do you understand that feeling?"

"I feel it every day. The coming of the new century was devastating to me for precisely that reason. I like to think of myself as a progressive man in many respects, yet I cannot escape the awareness of my statue-like tendencies. The world strikes me as an inherently selfish place. I am all for innovation and improvement, but at what cost? Why must it be forced on us before we are prepared for it? My apologies, I'm veering off-topic."

"That's alright," she said with a smile. The two stood in silence for a moment before Emily spoke again, the daylight almost extinguished now. "As a child, I used to sit by my bedroom window. I'd watch people pass by and notice how they'd be laughing or rushing, holding hands, or carrying parcels. Each time I spied them, I would think I must be invisible. That if they couldn't see me, then maybe I didn't exist. I've never confided this to anyone… not even Anne. But I think you understand, Hugo."

He did understand… and he did not. A more nuanced understanding would imply that while he thought he grasped it, the reality was far more complex. For Emily, being seen by others would have improved her condition, but for Hugo, although he constantly yearned for human connection—to be seen for his true nature and innate talents—he was fussy beyond irrationality. Hugo did not desire to be perceived by mundane populace; he cared only for the exceptional. That was where the two diverged so intensely.

There was one thing Emily had said that beckoned him, something he knew he could not resist asking about. A seemingly unintentional remark, quickly regretted. "Anne?"

Emily avoided looking at him for a moment, and he could sense her inner turmoil. "She was my dearest friend. When she left, I seemed to vanish from the world entirely."

Hugo wanted to press the issue. A ravenous curiosity now consumed him—so badly did he want to inquire about Anne's fate, what their friendship had been like, and the nature of the conversations they once shared. But he could sense he was treading on treacherous ground. There was an unmistakable depth of pain and longing reflected in Emily's eyes when that name had slipped from her lips. So, he said nothing.

"This may be improper of me…" Emily said, her hesitation clear. "Would you like to come inside?"

CHAPTER EIGHT
Anne

The first thing that struck him was how the room clung to the last remnants of light. The sun had long since dipped below the horizon, leaving only the faintest trace of its glow—a pale, silvery sheen that bled through the tall windows. It barely illuminated the space, casting shadows that pooled thickly in the corners and stretched jaggedly across the walls. In the brief pause before nightfall, the room appeared caught, still, as if anticipating something, suspended between light and dark. Dust floated in the dimness, visible only when it crossed the narrow paths of dying light.

Though the room's shadows were oppressive, Emily moved through it as though she carried her own light. To Hugo, it was not only the manner in which she struck a match and lit the oil lamp on the table, casting a small circle of flickering warmth; it was the way she moved next to the mantel to light a pair of candles, then crossed to the far corner to ignite a second lamp near her easel. Slowly, her touch softened the room, the golden light coalescing in every corner until she banished the shadows. It was not just the light that transformed the space, but Emily herself. Hugo thought that she completely filled the room, as if her presence was woven into the canvas and the brushstrokes on the walls. To him, she was the room's very heartbeat.

The small apartment now lit, Hugo's eyes ran over the walls, decorated with artwork that seemed oddly familiar. Landscapes hung above the mantel—rolling hills that warped at the edges, their trees too tall and twisted to be real. A painting of the Thames caught his eye, its waters rendered in shimmering green and gold, as if the river were molten glass. Beside it hung a portrait of a man with piercing eyes that seemed to follow Hugo as he moved.

The furniture was simple, infused with a tiredness that spoke of better days. A low wooden table sat in the centre of the room, its surface scratched and scattered with charcoal sticks and scraps of paper. Near the fireplace slumped a faded armchair, its upholstery fraying at the edges, while a modest bookshelf stood in the corner, its contents leaning unsystematically as though unsure of their place.

Everywhere Hugo looked, he saw signs of Emily's presence. A half-finished canvas propped against the wall depicted a street scene he recognised but could not name. On the nearby easel stood another painting, this one of a garden drowned in shadow, the trees bending towards each other like conspirators—he would have sworn that they were whispering.

"This is me," Emily said, breaking the silence. Her voice was soft, almost apologetic. She set her things down on the table, brushing a stray strand of hair from her face. "I know, it's… not much."

Hugo shook his head, his eyes lingering on a row of more miniature portraits along the far wall. "It's… alive. Every piece here… they each have a story waiting to be told."

Emily's lips curved into a smile, but she did not respond. Instead, she gestured towards the armchair. "Please, sit. I'll prepare some tea."

Fearful of sullying the room's holiness, Hugo proceeded with painstaking slowness. As he lowered himself into the chair, a small portrait propped against the mantel caught his attention. It differed from the others—simpler, smaller, but far more intimate.

The subject of the painting was a young girl—no older than sixteen, he thought—her fair hair loose around her shoulders. She stood in the heart of a field, her eyes bright but distant, as though looking at something just beyond the frame. The scene blurred at the edges, as if fading into memory.

"Who is she?" Hugo asked, hearing Emily return from the kitchen. He must have been staring at the portrait for longer than he had realised, as Emily had now entered the room holding a teapot in her hands. She paused when she saw what he was looking at, and her smile faltered. She briefly seemed lost another world.

"That's Anne," she said, her voice delicately woven with both fondness and sadness as she set the teapot down on the table. Hugo looked up at her; their eyes met while unspoken questions hung between them. "My best friend. She... died. A long time ago, when we were still so young. I painted that years later; it's the only way I could remember her properly."

Hugo turned his attention back to the portrait, observing the girl's face. He reflected on the surrounding paintings, and of the work he had seen in Emily's sketchbook—all those surreal, dreamlike landscapes and strange, distorted figures. He realised this piece was different. This painting was not just art; it was a memory, immortalised in oil and canvas.

"She looks happy."

Emily let out a gentle breath, a sound that was not quite a laugh. "She was," she said before sitting down. "Happier than anyone I've ever known. Nothing like either of us."

Hugo nodded, uncertain of just what he should say. A second glance at the painting yielded a newfound comprehension of Emily. "Tell me about her."

"She was my everything." Emily poured them both some tea from the teapot, then she fetched an aged sketchbook from the bookcase. The book was smaller than the one she'd shown before, and far more timeworn. She thumbed through the pages until she eventually stopped on one near the end of the book. "Here," she said, handing it over to him.

"It's her," he remarked, staring down at the rough sketch of Emily's lost friend. The style differed greatly from her more recent work—less sophisticated, oozing a rawness that could only stem from her younger self.

"I used to sketch her all the time. Flip back some pages—you'll see. She thought it was magic—the way I captured her contagious smile. After she passed, I couldn't draw for years. It felt... wrong—like I had stolen something from her. That's when I took up painting. I began to exaggerate things... change reality."

"You didn't steal anything."

"Of course not. But try imparting that wisdom to a distraught young girl. Back then, I felt like I had drawn her out of the world, trapping her onto paper. I cried every night. It felt like she was waiting for me to bring her back."

"Yet now... you sketch again, but you do not paint."

"It's complicated."

The two said nothing for some time, each immersed in their thoughts, sipping on their tea. Hugo was still desperate to know the answer to one specific question, but he did not have to ask it.

"Anne was so full of life, like you wouldn't believe. To this day, she remains the kindest person I've ever known. She was the only one who ever truly saw me—the sister I wished I had had. She was also stubborn. So incredibly stubborn. When she got sick... you should have seen her. She was never just a light in the dark; she was the ember that refused to go out, adamant and burning even as the ashes fell. I've always wished I could carry even a tiny fragment of her flame."

"She sounds special."

"She was."

They finished their tea in silence, entrenched in their own reflections once more. Eventually, Hugo was the one to break through the quiet. "Forgive me for asking this—it is not the most mannerly thing—but do you have anything stronger?" he gestured towards his empty teacup.

"Stronger tea?"

"No... stronger. Something more potent."

"Oh," Emily realised. "I'm not one to indulge in such vices very often. Earlier, I cited my father... he often went too far."

"I understand," Hugo nodded. "No matter."

"No, wait," Emily stood up abruptly, "I believe I have something." With that, she sauntered off towards the kitchen, and as he remained in his seat, Hugo could hear the gentle cacophony of her rummaging through cabinets. Eventually, she returned, carrying a bottle and two glasses. "Brandy," she declared.

"My favourite," Hugo watched as she poured a generous measure of the alcohol into both glasses. "I thought you were saying you didn't indulge..."

"I don't do it often. But I think the occasion calls for it." She sat the bottle down and handed a glass to Hugo.

"To Anne," he proposed, lifting his glass in a toast, and as he did, he saw Emily's eyes instantly well up.

"To Anne," she echoed quietly, trying to conceal the sorrow in her voice. She downed the whole glass in one gulp, much faster than Hugo did, then poured them both another. "Wait, don't you have to work tomorrow?"

Hugo chuckled, dismissing it as trivial. "I am experienced with this." His jovial declaration seemed to make her sad, as though reminding her of something she had been through before... many times before. Still, they continued to drink together.

"Earlier, you were drawing something, and when I approached, you hid it from me."

"I did, and I promised I'd show it to you when it's ready, which it's not."

"Can I just ask—"

"No."

"You don't even know what I was going to ask!" Hugo protested.

"I posses a rather astute intuition regarding your unspoken thoughts. The answer, however, is no—it's not a depiction of you. That's unnecessary, I think. I illustrate people only in moments when my words betray me. I guess I find it easier to make them sit still on paper than in reality. We aren't there yet."

"What do you mean?"

"Everyone leaves, Hugo. Sometimes, it's physical; other times, it's in spirit. My father, Anne, Francis… and eventually even you. I know you will. You can't help it."

"I do not plan on being buried any time soon, dear Emily, and barring such circumstances, I do not intend on parting ways with you so easily."

"Oh, Hugo…" she moved close to him, looking at him with all the empathy and intensity she could muster. Her words were almost prophetic; her spirit was pleading with his. "There are forms of death that transcend burial. I may not have known you long, but I can feel your soul—it's the kind that gravitates towards suffering, yearning to encounter pain wherever it can find it, for it is therein you might feel something real."

He reached out and took her hand in his, lifting it to brush against his cheek. Her skin felt so soft against his, contrasting starkly with the heaviness of their conversation. "If I am destined to suffer, then, dear Emily, permit it to be at your merciful hands."

CHAPTER NINE
The Cat

Hugo wavered in the doorway to his living room… though it wasn't quite his flat. The walls appeared too confining, the light appeared too weak, and the furniture seemed burdensome, as if someone had rooted it into the floorboards.

At the centre of the room, sprawled languidly across the rug, lay a cat. Its thick and dishevelled fur was the colour of ash, while its body stretched far longer than any house cat ought to. It lay there, still, save for the slow, rhythmic flick of its tail. Its yellow eyes were half-lidded and unreadable.

Hugo stepped into the room, crouching down to the cat's level. He stretched out its hand, curling and uncurling his fingers in a gesture meant to provoke some sort of reaction, but the cat simply blinked and turned away its head, unbothered and uninterested.

"Komm schon," he said in his native tongue, the softness of his voice muffled, as if swallowed by the air around him. He reached out again, this time brushing the tops of his fingers against the cat's warm, velvety fur. He sensed life beneath his touch, though the cat itself might as well have been carved from stone—it was a monument, a silent thing that refused to yield to him.

"Do something," Hugo said, his tone sharpened with

frustration. "Please…" The cat remained indifferent, still looking off to the far wall, dismissing him entirely.

It was then that a flicker of movement caught Hugo's eye—a darting shadow at the fringe of the rug. Then another… and another. Rats. Small and obsidian, their eyes glinted like shards of coal as they darted along the room's outskirts, disappearing into the dark crevices.

Hugo rose, a sudden, irrational fury welling up within. "They're under the couch," he said, and that was when the cat finally shifted. Slow and deliberate, as though the effort weighed it down, each step it took seemed impossibly heavy, as if the floor were struggling to bear its weight. It moved towards the couch, silent and unrelenting.

Urgently and purposefully, Hugo grasped the couch arm and shoved. Like nails on a chalkboard, the legs screeched against the floor as he moved it aside, revealing a nest of shadows beneath it. The rats froze for a single heartbeat, their tiny bodies quivering, and then they began to scatter.

The cat lunged. Its paws landed with lethal precision, and its jaws snapped with a sharp finality, utterly devoid of mercy. One by one, the cat seized the rats, cutting short their shrill squeals with its unyielding grip. Hugo watched on, transfixed, as the pile of lifeless shadows grew at his feet.

With the last rat dealt with, the cat sat back on its haunches, licking its paws with the same detached apathy it had displayed from the start. Then, it fixed its piercing yellow eyes on Hugo, wide and unblinking—almost mocking him.

"Is that all?" Hugo asked, his mind struggling to process how he'd have to clean up the mess. He crouched again, tentatively reaching out towards the cat once more. "What do you want from me?" he asked, but the cat did not flinch. Its gaze bore into him, unwavering, as though it were waiting for him to understand something he had not yet grasped. The silence between them was deafening.

It was then that Hugo realised the room was now empty. Furniture, walls, light—gone in a flash. He was adrift, accompanied only by the dead rats, and the cat, stranded in a boundless void.

He looked down at his hands, observing the crimson stains that seeped into the creases of his palms. The cat remained still, its eyes frozen with purpose.

Hugo woke up panting, a sense of desperation engulfing him, and a weight in his chest that refused to leave. "I suppose it's another one of those nights," he said to himself, dragging his weary frame from his bed towards the brandy.

CHAPTER TEN
Fire

It had been two days since that night they had spent together, and in that time, there couldn't have been as much as a ten-minute stretch that had elapsed without Hugo's thoughts succumbing to the memory of Emily. He was bewitched, and so when he returned to the garden the day following that night, he was immeasurably disheartened to be met with the sight of an empty bench. His mind, in disarray, raced for answers, some more logical than others. Ultimately, he clung to the notion that she had indulged too liberally in the brandy—she had told him she rarely partook, after all.

But when Hugo returned to the garden at lunch again the day after that, his efforts to devise reasonable explanations began to falter. For a second day in a row, the girl who was always in the garden was nowhere to be seen. He told himself that he'd return after work that evening, hoping that just maybe he'd find her then.

The oppressive wheels of time were hard on him that day. The merciless ticking of the office clock seemed slower than it had ever been before. To compound his torment, his workload was reaching unbearable levels. He had made little of a dent in any of it those past two days, and he was beginning to draw concerned looks from colleagues seated at neighbouring desks.

He found himself unable to focus on anything, no matter what he did. The singular obsession able to dominate his mind was Emily. Everywhere he looked, every word that reached his ears, each place he ended up, everything drew his thoughts back to her. Even in moments of attempted refuge—when he closed his eyes and tried to shut out the world—she lingered like the afterimage of something too bright to look at directly. Her scent—soft and fleeting, like wildflowers pressed into a book and forgotten for years—wasn't the kind of thing one noticed immediately, but rather, it was something that remained, subtle yet insistent, creeping into his awareness long after she had gone.

Her voice was a sound he could not escape. Low, warm, and unhurried, with a timbre that folded the air around it. Her delivery, just as much as her words, spoke volumes. Words that tumbled out as though they had been resting on her tongue for years. He perceived a strange, lilting quality in her tone, as if she were always poised between laughter and sighing.

On recollection, her delicate but restless hands struck him the most. As she spoke, they sketched soft lines in the air with constant movement—a gentle choreography of thought and expression. He thought of how they ought to feel—cold against his skin, or perhaps warm, depending on the day. Her fingers smudged with charcoal would have been more intimate than any touch, leaving faint traces of her creativity across everything she handled.

That loose, dark hair fell in careless waves that did not just defy gravity but actively challenged it—curling and twisting with a life of their own. He imagined smelling it, of burying his face in it, of it wrapping around his fingers like ivy—soft and endless, refusing to let go.

But her eyes enthralled him above all else. Those large, contemplative, deep pools of azure were not overtly remarkable for their hue, but there was something in how she looked at things, at people... at him. She could see through a person's layers, peeling them back like paper to expose what lay beneath—that terrified Hugo as much as it thrilled him.

Even the way she moved haunted his memories. She carried herself with the quietest of energies, her posture never quite right, a conflicted sense that she was constantly avoiding the confines of the human experience. She had a way of making the ordinary become extraordinary: the tilt of her head when she listened, the way her lips quirked to one side when she was concentrating, the faint furrow in her brow when she thought no one was watching.

Hugo's obsession did not end there; for he found himself captivated by even the most idiosyncratic of details. He noticed the way her breath would catch when she was startled, the faint tapping of her pencil against paper when her thoughts wandered, and the almost imperceptible way she bit the inside of her cheek when she was deep in thought.

And then there was her art. Her paintings were an essence made visible, surreal and disjointed, yet achingly precise. He thought of the landscapes she put to canvas, twisting and contorting at impossible angles, trees gnarled like ancient hands. Each piece appeared a fragment of her soul laid bare, stunning and unsettling in equal measure.

There existed moments where he had to gasp for air, overwhelmed by the crushing weight of her being. She was his ultimate paradox—grounded yet ethereal, distant yet close, fake yet real. His obsession eclipsed mere admiration; it was suffocating, all-consuming, and an ache he could not name. She had settled in the marrow of his bones.

When the workday finally ended, Hugo could not decide whether he should experience relief. On one hand, his agonising wait was over, but on the other, he now had to prepare for the possibility that the bench would still be empty.

It was.

Hugo sat alone on the bench for a long time, pondering whether he should try visiting her at home. In the end, he kept his distance, opting for yet another night of swallowing brandy with his shadow.

The following day at work was the worst yet. A persistent ache throbbed at his temples, his eyes were heavy, and his throat felt dry. These restless nights were catching up with him. At least, that's what he told himself, even if the truth lay more squarely with the bottle that had become his confidant. The office manager interrupted Hugo ten minutes before his lunch break, requesting a private conversation.

As Hugo reluctantly rose, fate itself intervened. "Fire!" yelled one of his colleagues from the other side of the room. Everyone leapt up to look out the window and see for themselves what was happening.

Beyond distant rooftops, several streets away, flame tore open the sky, thick dark smoke rising like accusatory fingers toward the heavens. An infernal blaze was wreaking havoc upon the city. "The garden…" Hugo whispered to himself, the grim reality dawning on him just where the fire was raging.

CHAPTER ELEVEN
At War with the Universe

Hugo flung himself into the chaos, not stopping to think twice about the conversation he was supposed to be having back at work. His heart hammered against his ribcage, threatening to escape. He had to get to the garden; he had to find Emily.

It seemed biblical that the fire was raging from the direction of the garden where Emily had invested so much of her time and spirit. He was so confused—he couldn't fathom why she hadn't been back there yet. Their last meeting had unfolded with so much promise.

Each step he took, the queasier he became—the most heinous, worst-case scenarios playing out endlessly in his mind. What if something had happened to her? If it had, he wasn't sure that was a reality he could face.

Hugo's shoes pounded against the cobblestones with urgency. He was in the thick of it now. Pressing forward, acrid smoke stung his eyes and clawed at his throat. He pulled his collar up over his nose and mouth, but it did little to shield him. Mayhem pulsed through the streets as panicked voices rose, horses reared in fright, and people frantically passed buckets in a line that felt more symbolic than practical. Every step brought him closer to the garden, but the overpowering stench of burning ash almost suffocated him, and the searing heat of the blaze licked at his skin, even at a distance.

Then he saw it—not the garden itself, but the row of buildings beside it, consumed by insatiable roaring flames. The inferno had already claimed the upper floors, windows vomiting fire and smoke into the noon sky, weaving a grotesque tapestry of destruction. The structures sagged under their own weight, timbers groaning like dying animals, threatening to collapse with each passing moment.

Hugo staggered, coming to an abrupt halt. His chest heaved as he looked on at the devastation. For a moment, he would have sworn he had seen the exact scene somewhere before. The flames writhed and twisted like living things, their shapes almost human, clawing and grasping in all directions without prejudice. They made him think of Emily's artwork—authentic, but with whispers of the surreal.

The colours were also hers: the searing orange of the fire, the oily black of the smoke, and the faint glimmers of gold that danced through the chaos like momentary sparks of hope. He almost felt guilty for thinking it, but it was a beautiful sight.

Sufficient destruction witnessed, he turned his attention towards the garden where he and Emily had first met, the place where they had forged the connection he felt so strongly now. Through the thick curtain of smoke, he could just make out its familiar outline—the low stone wall that bordered it, and the wrought-iron gate that creaked when pushed open. Shrouded in the dim unnatural glow of the flames devouring the building nearby, the garden looked to be unharmed. Hugo felt relief surge through him, so sudden and sharp that it somehow put even more pressure on his chest.

But the fire seemed to mock his relief, its infernal roar echoing in his ears like malicious laughter. Then came the thought, unbidden and cruel: what if this fire was theirs?

The garden, upon Hugo's arrival, was serene and untouched, ironically mocking his panic, just as the fire had mocked his brief respite. For a moment, he considered the possibility that the universe was at war with him. The garden seemed to have waited for him, muted and unchanged, but it felt distant, for yet again, Emily was not there. Behind him, the fire raged on, its heat curling around him like an unspoken truth he was not yet ready to face.

CHAPTER TWELVE
Masks

Hugo could no longer restrain himself, not after what had just happened. Uncertainty haunted him—how would she react? But he had to know Emily was alright. He knew that he would likely come to rue his decision, but the demands of his occupation were the last thing on his mind, leaving him no choice but to forgo his return from lunch, instead deciding to go to her. The whole time he walked, he could not dispel the impression that the fire near the garden had taken something from him—something intangible.

A smile touched her lips as she opened the door. Yet it belonged to someone else—someone he barely recognised. Hugo entered and took a seat with her in the living room. A quick glance around revealed an upsetting difference. The walls exhibited scars; stripped of the artwork that had once adorned them. Various trinkets that had been lying around just a few nights before were now nowhere to be seen. In the corner, he noticed a box.

"Going away…" he muttered, half asking a question, half observing in disbelief.

"Shouldn't you be at work at this hour?" Emily asked, her voice lacking its usual warmth. Something about her tone made him feel he'd done something wrong, but he did not know what.

"I... left early," he said, trying to wrap his head around what he was seeing. "There was a fire."

"A fire?!" Emily's expression shifted to one of worry. "Where? Is everyone okay?"

"I cannot say. It occurred near the garden where we usually meet. I was just there... searching for you."

"Oh..." Emily avoided meeting his eye. She kept readjusting her posture, her unease manifesting in her body language no matter how she positioned herself.

Hugo couldn't explain it, but every word they exchanged felt like part of a sombre dance—a dance where every step was leading them further apart, though neither of them seemed to be able to stop moving.

"Are you going somewhere?" Hugo asked, gesturing to the box in the corner.

"Oh, um, yes... I am."

"Where?"

Her face hardened like cracked stone as she answered. "To my parents."

"When will you return?"

"I shan't," she said, and for the slightest moment, he perceived the tremor in her bottom lip.

"I'm having trouble grasping... you told me that—"

Sharp and anguished, she cut him off: "I know what I told you." "Sometimes fate unfolds in a cruel way, Hugo. Things don't always go the way you desire them to. That's life."

"What happened? I thought your sister—"

"She can't help me anymore! She simply cannot, okay? I'm sorry for yelling, but this is just how it is. It's all over for me."

"Oh, dear Emily, please, I implore you—let me help you."

"Help me? Employ some realism for a moment, Hugo, will you?"

"I mean it. I can help, I can—"

"You can what? Provide for me? Even if I were to concede on that point, why would you do such a thing? What motivation would push you to such an act of kindness? I will not be an object of your charity, nor will I be your whore."

"My... oh, no, you misunderstand. That's not what I'm saying at all."

"Then what, pray tell, are you saying, Hugo?"

At that moment, if Emily had asked him to die, he would have. Hugo would have surrendered himself to her entirely, no matter what she asked of him. His deepest desire was to bare his heart to her, and he yearned for her to reach out and take it in her hand. If she had crushed it there and then, that would have been alright, for right then, in her living room, he had decided that being devoured by her was the only thing he had ever wanted.

But Hugo Henke was not real, and so he could not go all the way.

"I care for you," he finally said, breaking through an agonising momentary silence.

"You care for me? Hugo, you barely know me, and I know you even less. How long has it been since we met? A week, maybe less? How can you dare to profess to know me, let alone care for me?"

"But the things we spoke of… the things you told me that night…" Hugo strained to contain the raging emotions that threatened to obliterate him, feeling an overwhelming avalanche welling up in his eyes. It took everything he had not to flood the entire room.

"You think that my anecdotes of loss… that me telling you about the death of my friend… mean that we should live together in bliss? You don't even know my last name."

Hugo had never seen Emily like this. He didn't even believe it was really her. It felt a lot like she had put on a mask, now performing some ritualistic dance to repel him at all costs. Despite his best efforts, he could not understand it. "No, you've misunderstood me," he argued, but the chasm had already grown too deep.

"Then what?"

Hugo had crossed far beyond simple discomfort. The intensity of Emily's aggression was so shocking and unforeseen that he sensed a retreat into silence beginning. The more he wrestled with his genuine feelings for her, the worse it became—he found himself incapable of formulating coherent thoughts. And so, unable to deal with what it took to be real, Hugo Henke accepted he was not. "You are running away. That's all this is."

Her appearance transformed before him, filling out, expertly taking on the full shape of the mask she had been donning. To say she was unpleased would have been a gross understatement. "And what are you doing, Hugo? Staying put and calling it courage? Don't fool yourself."

"I'm trying to hold on to something, Emily. Can you not see that?"

"No, you're trying to clutch at me as if I'm some lifeline that exists to save you from drowning. I cannot be that for you. I will not."

Despite his own mask, her words cut him deep, deeper than any knife could have. Most disheartening was that she was right—he really was neck deep in water, offering her his hand as though it were of any use. Hugo's tone turned harsher. "You're leaving, just like you accused everyone else of doing."

"And maybe there's a reason for that."

The culmination of their back-and-forth felt like the snapping of a violin string. Tension released in an instant, leaving behind an echo of something irrevocably fractured.

"Then, dear Emily, I bid you farewell."

CHAPTER THIRTEEN
Spilled Ink

He couldn't sleep at all that night, but for a change, the thought of reaching for a drink repulsed him. By the time the faintest hints of light crept through the curtains, he could no longer bear the restless toss and turn. He pulled on his coat and stepped out into the fog-laden streets, the air cool and damp against his skin.

Such insidious fog in summer was somewhat unusual—it was as though the city itself had exhaled some long-held breath and refused to take it back. The cobblestones gleamed under his feet, their slick surfaces catching the faint glow of the rising sun. London appeared forsaken, every sound muffled by the mist that curled around corners and crept into alleyways.

Hugo wandered without direction, his feet moving of their own accord. He told himself that he was walking to clear his head—to impose order on the chaos that ruled his thoughts—but the truth was, he feared the stillness of any other choice. He was not ready to confront his despair. Despite the erratic rhythm of his footsteps, they provided him with an anchor amid the storm of his mind.

Thoughts of her besieged his consciousness. Her voice held firm within him, rising and falling with a rawness that did not belong to her at all. He thought of her large eyes—how they had transformed from something magical to something hardened, like cold stone. He recalled her words, each one an unseen injury, its presence pervasive.

Before he realised it, he approached the garden. The low stone wall emerged first as a ghostly outline in the fog, and then the gate, followed by the shapes of some distant trees. He hesitated at the entrance, and for a moment, he considered turning around. This place, once a sanctuary, now felt hollow, a shell of what it once represented. But then he saw the figure.

Faint at first, hardly visible through the mist, but unmistakable. A flash of red, stark against the dullness of the morning. His breath caught in his throat, and he instinctively stepped behind the gatepost. Squinting into the obscurity, he discerned her—Emily, standing by the bench.

She was alone; her figure softly outlined by the glow of the morning sun beginning to break through the fog. She moved quickly, as if in a hurry, her hands fumbling with something in her grasp—an envelope.

Part of him wanted to dash over to her and somehow undo everything that had been said the night before, but that part held no authority over the rest of him. After all, he was not real. So, he hung back, frozen not only by the sight of her, but by a sense of longing.

She looked smaller to him somehow, less sure than she usually did. He watched as she stooped—the red of her coat pooling around her like spilled ink—and attached the envelope to the bench's armrest. She stayed for a moment; her head bowed slightly, and then she turned and walked away. Like a wraith, she dissolved into the mist.

Hugo lingered by the gate for a while longer, his heart racing as he considered the potential contents of the envelope. He advanced, his steps cautious and deliberate as he crept along the path towards the familiar bench. Emily had secured the envelope to the wood; his name was written on it in her unmistakable handwriting.

His fingers trembled as he reached for it, and as he pulled it free, he could not avoid the thought that it might crumble away at any second. He chose not to open it right away. Instead, he settled down on the bench, his eyes fixed on the envelope as the surrounding fog began to lift. He traced the edges of the paper with his thumb, his heart a tangled mess of hope and dread. Whatever this was... whatever she had left for him... it was all that remained.

For the first time in hours, he let himself breathe.

CHAPTER FOURTEEN
Paper and Ink

Should he have allowed the tears to flow? Perhaps they might have possessed the power to cleanse his soul. It may have been worthwhile, even if their cessation was unlikely. They could have snuffed out the sun itself, but at least Hugo might have found some semblance of peace. In the end, the floodgates remained sealed, but that did not prevent the rain from striking his window from the world beyond his flat. Soft, yet insistent, the city reflected his deep, unexpressed anguish, mourning with him.

He sat slouched at the foot of his bed, surrounded by the clutter of his measly existence. In his unsteady hand, he clutched the contents of Emily's mysterious envelope, which he had been clutching for hours. Hugo had kept the envelope sealed until he returned home, and then he spent the better part of an hour just staring at it, dreading what he might find inside. When at last he pried it open, he extracted a folded sheet of paper. On the back were two words written in soft pencil: *I promised.*

His hands had quivered as he unfolded the drawing; it had been as though he thought it might disintegrate under his touch. Emily's artistry—a perfect balance of bold, delicate lines, precision, and whimsy—was unmistakable. The scene she had depicted was so unbearably warm, and as he cradled the paper, he knew he could never let it go. It was a landscape so distant, yet inexplicably familiar. Rolling hills stretched towards the horizon, their curves impossibly smooth, and the grass that covered them shimmered like silk under an unseen sun.

At the centre of the drawing stood a church, its steeple bent at an angle, making it look like it was literally bowing in prayer. The windows had a faint glow, as though they were lit from within by something that was alive. The door, ajar, revealed a suggestion of a face—a mouth perhaps, caught mid-sentence. Hugo could have sworn it was whispering to him from the paper.

In the foreground, animals massed together in unnatural clusters, their bodies half-real and half... something else. They conversed with one another as if they were people trapped in lesser forms. Birds perched on the shoulders of foxes—their wings spread wide as though caught in a perpetual flight—and a raven stood at the edge of a crystalline stream, her reflection distorted in the rippling water. Under a tree, a cat curled beneath the shade, though the tree had no leaves, only golden orbs that hummed with light. Just off to the side stood a rabbit, holding a single lavender rose between its teeth.

Strangely, the sky above it all affected Hugo the most. Immense and teeming with life, spirals of colour moved through it like living things beyond his comprehension, leaving the sky a mess that he could not name. He decided it was not a sky, but something else entirely—it was a dream of a sky, one that housed stories that would never be told.

In the bottom corner, faint against the grass, Emily had inscribed a single line, small: *I found where I went.*

Hugo remained at the foot of his bed for the remainder of the day, still sulking there even when the sun came up the morning after. He could not bring himself to let go of the drawing, and the thought of her clung to him, refusing to relinquish its hold over his soul; for he was a man of paper and ink—thin, fragile, and easily torn. She was something else, something stronger. Something real.

PART 2

AUTUMN

A Soul of Ash

CHAPTER FIFTEEN
Backward Through Time

The train rattled onward through the foggy morning, its rhythm uneven, as though the tracks themselves were unsure of the journey. Hugo slouched by the window, hunched into himself, his coat collar turned up against the cold draught that was creeping through the carriage. Beside him, the glass of the window was speckled with condensation, blurring the barren fields and skeletal trees that stretched into the distance. What little sunlight pierced the gloom arrived pallid and uninspiring, seeping pathetically through the window and into the carriage.

His reflection stared back at him in the glass, faint and distorted—a ghost imposed over the world outside—a world he cared little for. He thought it might have made for an interesting painting, but art had never been his thing. He shifted under his own ghostly gaze, turning and instead looking at the other passengers scattered throughout the carriage. A thin man in a tattered coat sat across from him, his head nodding forward as sleep threatened to claim him. Farther down, a woman rocked a crying infant, its screams irritating a restless older gentleman seated nearby. Hugo was doing his best to ignore the noise, but he had lacked patience as of late. He had become much more bitter than usual, and furious at the world.

Hugo turned back to the window, observing the outside

realm. The countryside rushed past, blurred, and colourless; its fields churned to mud, and the trees stripped bare. Autumn had claimed the land, its fiery hues painting a landscape of decaying leaves under a grey sky, a scene that seemed to wait in resignation for winter's finishing touch.

He ran his fingers over the worn fabric of his seat, noting the frayed edges and loose threads beneath his fingers. Though Hugo had never really enjoyed life, he had never felt as he did now—such an overbearing sense of decay. Everything seemed to be falling apart. The train, the land, himself—they were all singing the same song of loss.

His eyelids fluttered shut, then snapped open; he didn't deserve such peace—sleep had refused him. Instead, his mind returned to the interview from the week prior, the way the man across the desk had folded his grubby hands, his face lined with a faint amusement and something bordering on pity. Hugo had hated him from the moment he saw him.

The train jerked, pulling Hugo out from his thoughts. He shook himself off and looked out the window again, this time ignoring the scenery, instead watching water droplets run down the glass. They traced erratic paths, crossing and dividing, losing themselves in the pane's blur.

He remembered warmth; he remembered fire. At that moment, he wished the train would go up in flames; such a fate would have been preferable to what was happening now. Tethered to the past, he was being dragged backward through time.

This was not a journey, at least not in the way people intended journeys to be. It was an undoing. With each passing mile, Hugo sensed himself unravelling, each thought and sensation peeling away like layers of old yellow wallpaper, exposing the flawed foundation beneath. Hugo rested his forehead against the cold glass, his breath clouding it further. "Back to Berlin," he muttered to himself, though the clatter of the train swallowed his voice. He wasn't just travelling to Berlin; he was being reeled back into it.

The countryside rushing past the window twisted in strange ways—shapes rising and falling like warped folds of a collapsing dream. In the blur, Hugo swore he glimpsed outlines of things that should not have been there—a crooked house with a door that blinked like an eye, and a tree with roots that stretched too far upward and into the sky.

Time was faltering, showing itself for what Hugo had always suspected it of being—a charlatan. The minutes folded in on themselves, collapsing and expanding, until Hugo was unsure whether he'd been on the train for hours or days. He could feel the weight of his younger self somewhere in the distance, a boy wandering the halls of a house that always felt a little too cold.

As the train continued to rattle along the tracks, Hugo heard his father's voice thundering beneath it. Was this what he deserved? To return, to face the ruin of the life he had left behind. Perhaps the train was not a vehicle at all. Perhaps it served as a confession; a punishment; a reminder that existence was not a straight line but a circle—a trap that wound tighter the more you tried to resist it.

He closed his eyes again… and he felt like he was falling. The uneven rhythm of the wheels beat on, carrying him without mercy towards the place he had once fled, and further from the place he had once hoped would be his salvation. Hugo kept falling. Backward. Always backward.

CHAPTER SIXTEEN
The Interview

Suffocatingly cramped, the office was much smaller than what he was used to. The ceiling sagged, and yellow tinged, cracked plaster marred the walls. Shelves crowded the unattractive walls, crammed with papers and ledgers, their edges curling with age and dampness. Where shelves were absent, faded posters displayed outdated headlines. Ink and stale tobacco filled the air, clinging to everything like a second skin. Hugo had prepared himself, sworn that he'd suppress his bitterness, donning a front of courtesy and optimism—this was his last chance at employment. But Hugo couldn't help himself, for this disreputable newspaper was a mausoleum for shattered ambitions.

He sat opposite a stout, balding editor; it appeared someone had hastily glued on his patchy beard. Despite the cool weather, sweat stained his shirt, and his glasses slid down his nose as he peered at Hugo over the rims.

"So, Mr Henke," the man began, his voice heavy with a fatigue that seemed more existential than physical. "You're interested in our political correspondent position?"

"Yes," Hugo said, his voice coming out tight and fast, nerves betraying him. "I've worked with words most of my life." He had said little, but he could already sense the opportunity slipping away from him. It found such difficulty in feigning interest for something he felt so fiercely was beneath him.

The editor nodded absently, flipping through the thin pile of papers Hugo had given him—his curriculum vitae accompanied by some writing samples. "No mention of academic credentials?" the editor remarked, leaving Hugo unsure if it had been a statement or a question.

"I have no proof of it." Though outwardly calm, Hugo seethed with silent rage.

"And why, exactly, did you leave your last position?" the editor asked without looking up. "The date here indicates a termination two months hence."

"I—" Hugo faltered. He had rehearsed this answer a dozen times to himself, but the truth caught in his mouth like a splinter lodged in flesh. "There were... personal circumstances."

The editor raised an eyebrow, finally looking up at him over the papers. "Which party was responsible for the termination of your employment?"

"It was mutual."

"I see," he said, sounding unconvinced. "And those circumstances... they won't be a problem here?"

"No, I am ready to move forward."

The editor leaned back in his chair, fingers steepled beneath his unsightly beard—an unseemly crown for a man so self-assured. "You know, Mr Henke, this isn't exactly *The Times*. We don't print poetry or philosophical musings. It's purely facts and deadlines here, plain and simple. Do you think you're the sort of man who can handle that?"

Hugo stiffened at the stout fool's tone, but he forced himself to *sort of* smile. Just who did he think he was to question Hugo's abilities? "Of course," he said. "I understand the importance of structure and consistency."

The editor's lips twitched, likely suppressing a smile that wasn't kind. He glanced again at the papers before setting them down with deliberate care on the desk between them. "Your samples are strong," he said, though his tone lacked enthusiasm. "You've clearly got some talent. However," he paused, and a fire ignited in Hugo, starting from his toes.

"What?" Hugo asked, his voice much sharper than he had intended, akin to drawing a knife in a moment of impatience.

The editor sighed, removing his glasses, and rubbing at the bridge of his nose. Hugo wished he would just cut to the chase. "But I need someone reliable, Mr Henke. Someone steady. I have seen many talented men come through this office…" Hugo had to suppress a chuckle. Who among the gifted would deign to set foot in a place like this? He was only here because of the absence of his credentials, which were necessary to get him anywhere else. "…do you know what happens to most of them? They burn out. Talent, after all, only gets you so far, Mr Henke. Far more critical is the discipline required to back it up."

"You think I lack discipline?"

"I suspect that you're going through something, and whatever that burden may be, it is written all over you. It's in your voice, your hands, and even in the way you walked in here. You are ill-prepared for this, Mr Henke."

The words should have been a blow, but Hugo had no respect for the man. In fact, he thought he could use a good punch in the face. Hugo was not inherently a man of violence, but for a moment, the rage building inside of him almost leapt across the desk. "You don't know me," he responded.

"No, but I know men like you. I am all too familiar with how this story ends."

Hugo said nothing in response, and the editor took it upon himself to continue. "Based on your own records, you've been out of work for two months. Employers seek dependability, Mr Henke, not turbulence."

Inside, Hugo was holding back a storm. It enraged him to be lectured by such a man, as though he were some academic novice. Although he intended his words to remain an inner monologue, he spoke them aloud anyway. "If losing the one person you ever connected with constitutes 'turbulence,' then perhaps I must rethink my understanding of adversity."

"I would call it life, Mr Henke. And I'd call it an excuse. We need someone reliable, someone consistent."

"Reliability? Consistency? Are you hiring a writer or a metronome?"

"I would say the two are more alike than you'd think."

On his way out, Hugo set his eyes on a decrepit plant by the door. Its leaves were curled and brown, and a sharp pang struck his chest as he passed it. He didn't want to admit it, but the plight of the plant resonated with him; he was the plant, and the plant was him.

CHAPTER SEVENTEEN
Trudging Through Tar

The carriage ride to the scene of his childhood was silent, save for the creak of the wheels and the occasional cough from the coachman. Hugo stared out at the streets from inside, the familiar grey stone of the buildings rising like monuments to a life he thought he'd left in the past. The closer they got, the more his chest tightened—a hollow, angry ache spreading through him like a disease.

When the carriage finally came to a stop, he was reluctant, hesitating before stepping down. It loomed before him—his old home—its pale façade washed out in the feeble light of the late afternoon. It loomed larger than in his memory, though perhaps that was just a reflection of the feelings he harboured deep inside. Once radiant and proud, the windows were streaked with grime and neglect, their shutters hanging at odd angles. Once meticulously kept, the front garden was now a tangled mess of weeds and overgrowth. For a moment, he found himself thinking about the servants. Where were they? How could they have allowed his family home to end up in such a state? His mother—how he remembered her at least—would never have allowed the place to end up so unsightly.

The large gate protested with a squeal as he pushed it open. Then he inched his way along the overgrown path until he reached the front door. Before he could knock, the door was already creeping open. One of the servants stepped forward to greet him.

"Master Henke," she said as she bowed her head, "you're back." She looked older than he had expected her to, or perhaps just more tired. He wondered just what had happened in the years he'd been gone. A lot, it seemed.

Hugo did not respond right away. His eyes instead swept over the entry hall, his steps echoing in the cavernous space as he stepped past the servant and into the house. The air inside was heavy and stagnant, as though the house itself had surrendered to melancholy. Before him, the grand staircase loomed, its once polished bannister now dulled, splintering at the edges. "My mother…" he finally spoke.

The servant cleared her throat, a strange discomfort hanging in the air. "About that… there's something you should know."

Hugo just stared at her, the words failing to register at first.

She hesitated, wringing her hands. "Mrs Henke… your mother…" she began, her voice barely above a whisper, her eyes avoiding his, as if she was unwilling to confront the sorrow she was about to impart. "She passed away just over two weeks ago."

The words hovered in the open. Unreal. Hugo blinked; his expression was unmoving. "What?" he spoke, his voice flat and toneless, as if the very concept of loss had failed to breach his fortress of reason.

"She fell ill with pneumonia," the servant continued, her eyes stuck on the floor. "She had been unwell for quite some time. We did everything we could, but…"

He didn't hear the rest. The words blurred into a monotonous hum, the servant's voice dwindling into the hollow expanse of the house. Pneumonia. Dead. Two weeks prior. He felt like he was standing in a dream—no, a nightmare, the kind wherein the atmosphere is too thick, where every step forward feels like you're trudging through tar.

"She asked about you. Right up until the end. She asked if you would come."

"What did you tell her?"

"That you would. I didn't know what else to—"

"And my father?" Hugo interrupted, his voice cold and mechanical.

The servant flinched, then straightened her posture. "In his room. Shall I escort you to him?"

Hugo nodded once, not trusting himself to speak.

The walk through the house was both familiar and foreign. Each step dredged up memories he had long sought to entomb. The walls displayed portraits; their once-vivid colours now faded, the faces staring down at him with an indifference that almost felt alive. A rug in the hallway lay tattered and worn, its intricate pattern now obscured by a layer of dust.

"We were told not to touch anything," she said, noticing Hugo inspecting the place. "Months ago, when Mrs Henke first fell ill, your father decreed nothing was to be changed. He dismissed the new girl when he caught her trying to sweep the kitchen. Aside from preparing his meals, our presence has become redundant, yet he insists we stay."

"You're still being paid?" Hugo inquired.

"Of course," she confirmed.

"What happened at the funeral?" Hugo asked, in a tone so low that he was surprised she even heard him.

"There... hasn't been one, Master Henke."

Silence enveloped them, and Hugo asked no more questions.

They finally reached his father's bedroom door, and the servant knocked, her fingers lingering on the handle as if hesitant to venture further. "Mr Henke?" she called gently. "Your son has returned."

A muffled voice emanated from within, low and unintelligible. The servant hesitated, glancing back at Hugo. "He insists he is not to be disturbed. I can show you somewhere to wait—"

"No," Hugo cut her off. "I shall see my room."

The servant hesitated again, but eventually nodded, guiding him down another shadowy corridor. The air grew colder as they walked, and Hugo detected the faint odour of mildew creeping in. His room awaited him at the far end, the door ajar.

"Thank you," he told her. "I will manage from here."

As she retreated down the hallway, Hugo reflected on his life in London, a glaring contrast to his years spent in Germany. He once thought he had had it so easy in Germany; he had servants around to cater to his every whim, never going to bed hungry, and never having to want for anything. But that wasn't the whole truth. Although material wealth may have spoiled Hugo, the fundamental desires of his spirit remained unaddressed.

The one thing he had always wanted was the thing that no one could ever give him; a treasure beyond his reach—he yearned to be understood. Others might have deemed him a fool for it, but in an instant, Hugo would have surrendered his full belly and warm bed for just one moment of genuine connection.

When he left Berlin, he had no shortage of reservations. He worried about having to take care of himself, doing his own chores, and the precariousness of financial independence. But to his surprise, none of those things ended up bugging him that much. The freedom he had gained eclipsed the inconveniences which accompanied it. This liberation contributed to the painfulness of his return. It felt as though he had willingly refitted his own shackles.

As the servant finally disappeared from his view, he took a deep breath and thought of his mother, of the last time he had seen her. She had stood in this doorway with her arms crossed, her expression stern but her eyes soft with an unspeakable sorrow. She had not tried to stop him, and that unspoken acceptance wounded him most. He shook off the memory and stepped into his old room.

CHAPTER EIGHTEEN
The Room

Hugo pushed the door shut behind him with the heel of his boot, the faint click echoing in the stillness. The room seemed more confined than in his memory, though nothing at all had changed. Once a delicate pale yellow, the wallpaper had now faded, peeling, and curling at the edges like dying leaves. The mattress on the bed sagged in the middle, the metal frame chipped and rusted. Cobwebs gathered in the corners of the room, fine and frail, undisturbed by the draught that crept in through the window's loose frame.

The room stank of dust and neglect, but it carried a slight hint of something else, something familiar and a tad sour—an unsettling nostalgia. Hugo stood in the centre of the room, disbelief washing over him like an ice-cold wave. It all remained—frozen in time. The desk where he had once scribbled essays and letters, its surface scratched with years of restless energy. The bookshelf, a tad askew, still holding the same volumes that his father had once insisted he read—Greek philosophy, German history—the weight of the world pressed into the worn hardcovers. Even the curtains were the same, pale, and threadbare—their edges frayed as if nibbled at by creatures of time.

He let out a breath and sank onto the edge of the bed. The

mattress groaned beneath him; a sound that struck him as absurdly human. He stared over at the desk, at the chair tucked neatly beneath it, and for a moment, he saw himself sitting there, younger, and smaller, a boy with ink-stained fingers, his dreams too large for even this enormous house.

You will never amount to anything if you cannot even sit still. His father's sharp, scolding voice echoed in his head. The memory slammed into him with all the full force of the original moment, and he could almost perceive the heavy, constricting grip of his father's hand upon his shoulder—a pressure intended to correct, to control.

Hugo's jaw tightened as he leaned forward, his elbows resting on his knees. The anger bubbled up again, hot and restless, but the crushing reality of what he had just learned tempered it. His mother was gone. Repeating the words in his mind, he tried to force belief and acceptance, but to no avail. A consequence of his well-honed instincts, which had assisted him in slipping out from under his father's smothering influence. He had once sworn to himself that he would never again allow anyone to hold authority over his mind—an obvious lie.

Frieda had been so alive to him, even in the years of silence that followed his departure. His mother had always existed in his mind as something enduring—bitter and flawed, yes, but alive. The woman, who had possessed incredible strength, was now reduced to a memory, fragile as the dust motes that floated in the still air, each one a tiny speck of what had been.

Hugo sprang to his feet, the sudden motion leaving him unsteady for a moment. He crossed the room to the desk, which stuck as he tried to open it. A sharp tug forced it open, and inside, he found scraps of his childhood. A broken compass, a tin soldier missing its left arm, a crumpled ticket to a long-forgotten play. His fingers paused over each item before settling on something small and soft.

A swatch of fabric, folded into a neat square. He pulled it out and unfolded it, his breath catching when he recognised it. A delicate linen handkerchief, the embroidery of his initials barely visible against the creamy fabric. The stitching was faint; the threads loosening in places, but he could still make out the tiny flowers his mother had sewn into the corners.

He sank back down onto the bed, gripping the handkerchief in his hands. The fabric may have been thin, but it had a heavy presence, as though it carried the weight of her absence. His chest ached with a sudden, overwhelming force, and his vision blurred as tears spilled over, hot and unwelcome. No sound came from him, nor did he sob, yet his shoulders shook with the effort of holding it all in. He hated her for dying. He hated himself for leaving. He hated his father for sitting behind that door, unmoved by the son who had come back to him.

Finally, drained and trembling, Hugo lay back on the bed, curling onto his side like a child seeking the comfort of something long gone. A crack, a thin fissure like a scar, ran down the centre of the ceiling above him.

He clutched the handkerchief to his chest, his breathing erratic, his mind circling the same thoughts again and again. If only he had come back sooner. If only things had been different. If only he had been real.

That room had seen every version of him. The boy who loved, the boy who cried, the boy who hated, the boy who left. But it had not seen the man who returned. No one had. For the boy who had once dreamt of escape was long lost, and the man who had returned had not survived the journey.

CHAPTER NINETEEN
Ruins

Hugo opened his eyes. How long had it been? The dim evening light filtered through the window, cloaking the bedroom in shadow. He raised himself, his body stiffened by weariness, his head heavy, and nausea lingering.

For a moment, he didn't know where he was. The silence of the house surrounded him, so absolute it seemed wrong. Then, like the stiff wind rustling through the autumn leaves, it all came back to him—the train, the house, and the harrowing news about his mother.

He dragged one hand across his face, willing himself to focus. His eyes fell to the handkerchief still clutched in his hand, its edges crumpled, dampened with sweat. Clenching his teeth, he tucked it into his coat pocket before rising to his feet.

The hallway was dark, save for a slender shaft of light spilling out from a door at the far end. Hugo slipped out, his footsteps muffled by the worn rug. The air was much colder now, a chilling draught seeping through cracks in the old wood of the house. He moved towards the light, each step more tentative than the last, his heart pounding louder than his feet.

The door to his father's study was ajar. He paused; his hand poised near the handle. Curiosity, or perhaps something darker, drew him forward, and with a slow, deliberate motion, he pushed the door open, its hinges groaning in protest. His father was inside... but not quite.

Slumped in a large armchair, Hugo lay his eyes upon a statue worn smooth by time and tears. A toppled monument, a once imposing presence, diminished to rubble beneath the weight of grief. The dark locks that had once framed his face were now sparse and streaked with grey. His hands, once steady as stone, quivered as they rested upon the armrests. Hugo wondered how such changes were even possible in only a few years. How was it possible that the tides of time could reshape a man, leaving him almost unrecognisable?

Papers lay scattered across the desk beside him, a disorganised collection of letters, receipts, and photographs. Among them were a few objects Hugo recognised—his mother's comb, a small brooch she had always worn, and one of her pressed flowers she had kept in a book.

Heinrich didn't notice his son at first. Lost in one photograph, attention ensnared, his lips moved in a kind of silent incantation, his words trapped within his mind.

Hugo stood motionless at first, like a frightened infant. It took him too many attempts at mouthing words before something eventually came out. "Father," he finally spoke.

Heinrich flinched at the sudden sound, his head snapping up in an instant. His expression was blank for a second, as though he did not recognise his own son standing before him. Then his eyes narrowed, faint lines deepening around them as recognition struck him.

"You're awake," he said, his voice like gravel.

"You didn't come to see me." Hugo advanced further into the room.

"I said I was not to be disturbed." Heinrich's gaze returned to the photograph cradled in his palm.

Hugo clenched his fists, his anger rising within him. He struggled to get his words out. "I came all this way, and that is all you have to say?"

"What do you want me to say?" Heinrich asked, his voice edged with exhaustion.

Hugo crossed the room on unsteady legs, eventually coming

to a halt before his father, like a soldier awaiting battle. He had been dreading the moment for a long time, but equally, he had been yearning for it. All those years, he had rehearsed countless dialogues in his head, envisioning just what he would say to his father if they were to meet again. He had fantasised about how they would yell at one another, about how his father would scold him with his familiar tirades, and about how this time, he would be the one who walked away the victor. But this man was not Hugo's father, at least, not the one he remembered.

Hugo should have been relieved, but the opposite was true. His father's fragility and indifference only angered Hugo all the more. He had spent so much time in preparation for this moment—for genuine confrontation—and now that was being taken from him, just like everything else.

Heinrich let out a bitter laugh, though it sounded more like a sigh. "Ah, I see what this is. Listen, Hugo, I am too old for yelling. Too tired. Do you imagine I have been sitting here, carefully crafting the words I'd utter should you ever return?" He shook his head. "I have better things to do. Or I did, before…" he trailed off, his gaze falling to the brooch on the desk.

Hugo's entire body tightened, his teeth grinding in his mouth as he looked down at his father. "I'm here."

"You're here," his father repeated back, his eyes still fixed on the brooch. "Too late, of course. But you are here. Now you can leave again, just as you did before."

"I didn't come for you." Hugo thought he might vomit at any moment.

"No. You came for her, and she's gone."

The silence that followed was unbearable. Hugo paced to the window, staring out at the overgrown garden below. "I should have been here."

"Yes, you should have. But you were not."

Hugo turned back to confront him, his anger flaring, but he was still incapable of letting it out. "You drove me away. You and your endless demands. Your… your rules, your judgement. Do you think I always wished to leave?"

Heinrich didn't respond. Silence hung in the air for a long time until Hugo finally turned and stepped towards the door. "I think…" Heinrich stopped him. "I think you wanted to be free of me. And I do not blame you for it."

The words hit deeper than any shouting match could have. Hugo stared at his father, desperate as he searched for some sign of the man he had resented for so long, but all he could find was a shadow, a figure hollowed out by the pain of loss. Somehow, it made Hugo gather even more hatred in his heart.

"You do not get to absolve yourself. You do not get to sit there and say you don't blame me. No matter what you declare, I still blame you."

Heinrich met his son's gaze, his own eyes tired, but steady. "If it helps. But it won't change anything. She's gone, Hugo, and we are all that's left."

Hugo turned towards the door, and his voice finally steadied as he spoke. "You are not the man I remember."

"No. And you are not the boy I remember. In fact, I don't think you're my son at all. Perhaps that's for the best."

Hugo said nothing in response. He stepped out of the room, closing the door behind him with finality. For a moment, he stood in the corridor, his breath uneven, and his mind racing. He had come for a fight, but all he had found were ruins.

And the ruins were worse.

CHAPTER TWENTY
A Coward's Eulogy

The morning had an overcast sky, a sombre, pale grey that neither threatened rain nor promised sun. Hugo stood at the edge of the cemetery, his hands buried deep in the pockets of his overcoat, a futile barrier against the biting wind that slipped through his seams and chilled his very marrow. The world seemed thin, as worn out as Hugo himself.

A small group of mourners huddled near the open grave; their faces turned downward as if sorrow was holding them to the earth. The priest stood beside the casket, his voice steady and rehearsed as he recited passages that Hugo did not hear. His father was present, of course, though Hugo hardly even glanced at him. Heinrich's face was ashen, his eyes fixed on the chasm— a gaping wound carved into the earth.

The servants maintained a respectful distance, their expressions solemn but impassive. Hugo knew they had worked for weeks in silence, forbidden by his father to change anything in his environment. Heinrich had been delaying the inevitable, holding onto denial as though it might somehow bring his wife back to him. The grand family home, once a place of order, had decayed along with him—dust gathering on neglected surfaces, mess piling up on tabletops, the air stagnating with unspoken grief. Hugo doubted a funeral would have occurred without his return.

Hugo's stomach churned as he etched closer to the grave. He took in a deep breath, saturating his lungs with the smell of damp earth decaying leaves. There she was, her casket resting poised just above the open pit, its polished wood gleaming faintly in the weak light. The closer he got to her, the more his chest tightened, and he felt like he might collapse under the burden of grief and remorse.

He had not intended to speak, but the priest had asked, and his father remained silent. So, despite not wanting to, Hugo felt he had an obligation to say something in honour of his mother. Anything. As murmurs faded out and eyes turned towards him, Hugo stood at the precipice of the grave, staring down into its haunting depths. As much as he feared death, part of him wished it had been himself who was to be put to rest that day. Maybe then, at last, he would find some inner peace.

Hugo cleared his throat, his own voice sounding foreign to him. "My mother…" he began, his words slow and contemplative. "Oh… Mother. You waited for me, didn't you? Until the end. But I wasn't there. I couldn't be, for I was afraid. Afraid of what might wait for me here upon my return… afraid to look into your eyes again. I couldn't bear having to see the resentment or sorrow that lived inside. I feared Father would take action in light of my misdeeds, and I worried that I would have to face things I had so desperately chosen to forget. Yet, when I did return—only when I had no other choice—the reality I faced was far more severe than anything I could have anticipated.

"I loved you—in my way. And I hated you. You were bitter… spiteful… cold. You wanted more from me than I was ever capable of giving, and I hated you for that. But you were also the only one who ever looked at me with what struck me as genuine admiration. The only one who ever held me, as seldom as it may have been, and the only one who really seemed to believe in me. You used to look at me and say: 'You can be better.' I do not know if you meant those words sincerely or if they were just an expression of your ire towards the man I was becoming. But I believed you, and I hated you for that, too.

"And then there is him… he's here, standing by your grave

like a statue with cracks running through it. Do you see him? Oh, Mother, from heavens above, please tell me that you see this man—how utterly small he has become. I implore you to witness him. He broke me many times, and I know he broke you as well. Now, here we are, gathered around this gaping wound in the earth, pretending it's all okay. Pretending we can forgive him for what he has done. Or maybe it's that we are pretending we can forgive ourselves for not fighting harder.

"Instead of fighting, you chose to retreat. You let him have his way, and you left me to deal with his wrath. I guess life was easier for you that way. But by choosing that path, you betrayed my trust, and even though I regret it, that is why I, in turn, let you down. You never fought for me, and so when the time arrived for me to fight for you, I ran away instead. We were both weak—ruled by our vulnerabilities—but perhaps that is permissible. Not everyone becomes a courageous warrior.

"While I was away, I never wrote to you. I'll be honest... I never once thought to. Not long after I stepped foot in London, my life back home faded into the background of my memory. I had come from opulence, but I was astonished by how easily I adjusted to a more frugal way of life. Of course, I had my plunder to help at first. The little I seized from home did me wonders those first few months. But if I am to speak candidly, I never missed the servants, the grand meals, or the fancy clothes. All I ever required was the little box I chose to build my nest in. The darkness calmed me while the brandy soothed me. They became the parents I always wished I had.

"Three years... more than that. I was gone, adrift in absence. Only recently did I confide in a... well, a friend. Former friend, to be precise. Anyhow, I shared with her how I believe time is nothing more than a distasteful illusion. That's something I decided on while I was away. I challenge anyone to disagree with me. Time is nothing but a cruel joke. If Father Time were to manifest himself here and now, I would spit in his face without hesitation. Disrespect? No, that is his manifesto. Time after time, we are each robbed of precious moments. I will no longer stand for it, even if it leads me to madness.

"All I've ever wanted in life is to be understood. But no one has ever been able to give me that gift. I always believed it was a simple thing to ask for, yet is has proven utterly unobtainable. I recently believed I had finally received this elusive gift...but I was wrong again. I have come to believe that what I seek may very well be beyond my grasp, for I am not a man, but a grotesque amalgamation of bones, flesh, and dejection.

"Why do I continue to live? Why do I persist in this realm? Upon my return home to an unmendable world, I find myself stuck on this question; I have asked it to myself multiple times each day. What is the purpose of anything? What happened to the meaning I was promised? The truth is, I am my father's son. I am a coward, doomed to grapple with his own frailty. And so, as a coward, I shall continue to suffer without action.

I still hate you, Mother. I hate you more today than I ever have. I hate you for dying; for leaving me to rot in the dull light of this overcast day. I will never forgive you for it."

Hugo stopped there, but the truth was, he had not really said any of it. The fantasy resided within his mind. Hugo Henke yearned to utter those words; they would have been his, had he truly existed. But alas, he did not.

Hugo was still standing by the grave. His father, a few distant relatives, the household servants, and a few other faces he did not recognise were all staring at him, just waiting for him to say something.

His throat tightened, the silence around him grating, and then he forced the words out. "My mother was not perfect. None of us are. But she was... there. For a time. And I think... I think that mattered. I should have been there too."

It wasn't much of a eulogy, but it was all he could manage. He stepped back, his eyes fixed on the casket, dodging the glances of the others standing around him. He let the silence swallow him.

Moments later, the priest's voice broke through his thoughts, signalling the last rites. Workers lowered the casket into the earth; the ropes strained under its weight as it descended. Hugo felt his breath catch as his mother disappeared into her final resting place.

He stared down at the grave, the turned soil mounded beside it, just waiting to be shovelled in. The wounded earth lay raw and unhealed. Hugo wondered if it ever would be.

A hand fell upon his arm, and he jumped a little, startled by the unexpected touch. He turned to see the face of an elderly woman. Her face felt familiar to him, though the exact connection eluded him. Perhaps a distant cousin of his mother's? "She waited for you," the woman said, her voice shaking. "Even when she knew you would not come, she still waited."

Hugo did not reply. He couldn't. Words twisted inside of him, jagged and painful, lodging themselves in the space where his anger typically resided.

The wind picked up, and brittle leaves scattered across the cemetery. Hugo pulled his coat tighter around him, turning away from the grave. He did not look back.

CHAPTER TWENTY-ONE
Cracks in Amber

Hugo sat at the edge of his mother's writing desk, the heavy oak groaning under his weight. The room—her sanctuary—was eerily quiet. Lingering in the air was a subtle hint of lavender, overlaid by the smell of age and disuse. The window was ajar, allowing a gentle breeze to brush the edges of papers that had lain undisturbed for months.

Though hours had passed since the funeral, its weight remained heavy on his shoulders. Hugo had avoided his father afterwards, retreating to this space as though it might provide him with some manner of insight—or at least a brief reprieve.

The desk drawers resisted him at first, their wooden frames swollen with time and disuse. With a determined tug, the first drawer reluctantly gave way, unleashing a small cascade of loose papers and envelopes. Hugo began sifting through them with a sense of methodical detachment.

Bills. Receipts. Correspondence from neighbours and distant relatives, none of which were of any interest to him—he cared little for what these people gossiped about. He set them aside without reading them.

Beneath all of those, he discovered a small stack of documents bound by a weathered blue ribbon. He recognised them at once—his academic records. The folder still held his First

Staatsexamen certificate, its ink and embossing faintly smudged. Oh, how he'd so badly wished that he'd taken this with him when he left for London. His fingers traced over the embossed seal, evoking memories of the ceremony he hadn't bothered to attend. At the time, he had thought that his First Staatsexamen was a key to a door he had not yet found. Now, however, it felt more like a reminder of his unrealised potential.

Erstes Staatsexamen in Literaturwissenschaft, the paper declared, inciting Hugo's lips to twist into a bitter smile. The smile vanished, and he placed the records aside to continue digging into the desk's remnants.

The next drawer was heavier, its contents shifting with a dull thud as he pried it open. Inside, nestled among stacks of old journals and stray bits of ribbon, was a photograph. Hugo paused for a moment before pulling it free. The photograph, sepia-toned, showed curled and worn edges. It depicted a family: himself, a boy of no more than ten, standing stiff between his parents. His mother's face housed a thin smile, her hand hovering over his shoulder. Beside them, his father stood rigid, a slight gap separating him and Hugo—a space that felt far larger than it seemed. His expression was severe, his stance a fortress of disapproval.

Hugo studied the image for some time, his fingers brushing against the faded surface. The tension in their poses was unmistakable now, the cracks in their dynamic as visible as the creases in the photograph. It was, as Hugo bitterly thought, a moment preserved in amber, its fractures more revealing than its clarity.

He wondered how she had smiled in that way. How had she pretended everything was fine? He placed the photograph beside his academic records, shifting his attention to the next drawer.

The last drawer stuck the hardest, and Hugo had to brace himself against the desk to yank it open. Inside, tucked beneath a stack of yellowing stationery, was a letter. To his surprise, he found the envelope addressed to him in his mother's careful handwriting. His address in London was absent, which made sense—she had never known it.

He turned the envelope over in his hands, the paper fragile

but intact. Memories of the last envelope he had opened came flooding back to him, and it took almost everything he had to not lose himself in a sea of tears.

After a few long minutes, he had regained his composure, though his throat was still tight. He unfolded the letter, the writing inside revealing itself to be dense and deliberate.

Dear Hugo,

I have been meaning to write to you for some time now, though I fear that no assemblage of words will ever suffice. You are, of course, my son, my only child. Though you may not have always felt it, I have always loved you, and I have always been proud of you, even if I did not demonstrate that fact in the ways you might have needed.

You were always different. I always knew that. Even as a boy, you saw the world in ways I failed to comprehend, and I see now how my inability to meet you there—on your terms—only drove you further away from me. You were quiet but never empty. Your thoughts were always turning, always moving. I could see it in your eyes, though your father regularly mistook your curiosity for rebellion. It could not have helped that when your father made these mistakes, I did not offer you my support. For that, I am sorry. I just hope that you can understand that I had my reasons. Hurting you was never my intention; I just didn't know how to navigate such uncharted waters.

Your father, well… he has his own brand of affection—one that is often harsh and unyielding, often manifesting as cruelty and coldness. Please understand, however, that his intentions are not malevolent. He does care, albeit in his own flawed manner. Still, I regret I could not soften his edges or, at the very least, stand firmer against him in the times when it mattered most.

But you should know that we both loved you. Our love for you will never change, regardless of past words. Each of us loved you in the only ways we knew how. I concede it a long way from perfect, and I accept you may hate me for not being more than I was, for not giving you more. But please believe me when I say that I have always believed in you. I still do. You have a way of seeing things that others overlook. Hold on to that, even if the world does not reward you for it. Especially then.

I wish I could send this to you, but I do not know where you are now. It is my fervent hope that you are flourishing, living the life you rightfully deserve—the life I know you never could have had here. Sometimes, I like to imagine where you might be. I envision you with a loving wife and children.

It seems so fantastical, but I think it's just my way of imagining you happy.

This, I expect, you will never read, and at this point, I think I'm writing only for my own peace of mind. I hope you understand that leaving does not mean forgetting. I haven't forgotten you, Hugo. I am still here, waiting, hoping that one day you will come back.

You have always been more than he sees in you, Hugo. I hope you see it too.

With love, always
Your mother

The letter trembled in his grasp as he finished reading; the ink blurring as unshed tears welled in his eyes. He wanted to feel something—relief, gratitude, love—but all that came was an acrid frustration.

"She didn't understand me. She never did."

In Hugo's mind, her words, as well-meaning as they were, only highlighted just how far apart they had always been. She thought he had rebelled out of spite. She mistook his reticence for anger rather than fear. She thought her belief in him had mattered, but belief without understanding was a hollow, miserable, bloody thing.

He considered crushing the letter into a ball or tearing it into a million pieces. Instead, he folded it, returned it to the envelope, and placed it beside the photograph. The combination of the two—the frozen family and the unsent words—felt unbearably poignant.

A knock at the door startled him, and he turned to see a hesitant servant standing in the doorway, holding a tray with a pot of tea and a single, mismatched cup.

"You asked for something warm, Master Henke."

Hugo had forgotten he'd made the request, but he nodded anyway. "Thank you."

The servant set the tray on a nearby table and then hesitated for a moment before slipping out the door, leaving him alone once more.

He stared at the photograph, the letter, and the steaming teapot, all of which seemed to conspire against him. The air in the room felt heavier now, pressing against him from all sides.

With a sigh, he moved to the table and sank into a chair, then poured himself a cup of tea—though he didn't drink it. His hands rested motionless on the table, numbed by contemplation.

She waited for me, he thought, the words from both the letter and the funeral echoing in his mind. *And I didn't come.*

One last time, he reached for the photograph, his fingers brushing the edges. He scrutinised his younger self, trapped between two towering figures that loomed over him. He felt as though he were sinking into the image, into the amber, into the cracks.

Beside him, the tea languished in silence, growing cold—another victim of time.

CHAPTER TWENTY-TWO
Ash

The fire in the hearth cast a weak, flickering glow across the study, its embers collapsing inward like the remnants of a burnt out life. Hugo stood in the doorway, his hand gripping the frame as though the wood might anchor him. His father sat in his armchair, his figure silhouetted against the firelight, surrounded by papers and shadows.

For a moment, neither spoke. The air between them was thick with silence, broken only by the occasional crackle of the fire. Hugo stepped into the room, his boots loud against the wooden floor.

"We need to talk," Hugo said, his voice steady but low.

Heinrich didn't look up. His hands trembled on the armrests of his chair, though his face remained impassive. "I presumed we already had."

Hugo clenched his jaw. "Not about this."

Heinrich let out a deep exhaled, as if the weight of Hugo's words had physically struck him. He gestured towards the chair opposite him. "Then speak, if you must."

Hugo did not sit. He remained upright, his entire body rigid, arms clasped across his chest. The fire crackled again, casting a faint glow over his father's face. "I have been waiting to have this conversation since the day I left this house. Since the day I decided I could not be here any longer."

Heinrich's gaze shifted to the fire, its glow reflecting in his tired eyes. "And yet, you came back."

"I have spent my entire life trying to make sense of this—of you, of her, of myself. Now she is gone, and all I have left is you. So, I would appreciate it if you would actually attempt to hear what I have to say."

Heinrich leaned back in his chair, his head tilting as he studied his son. "I said you could speak."

Hugo drew in a sharp breath; his chest was as tight as it had ever been. Then, the words erupted from him as if of their own volition. "You broke me. Shattered her. You demanded everything and gave us nothing."

Heinrich's jaw stiffened, his knuckles turning white as he gripped the armrests of his chair. "Nothing?" he forced a provocative laugh. "I gave you everything. I did what I thought was right—what was necessary. The world isn't kind, Hugo. It is unyielding; it does not care about your feelings or your dreams. I was preparing you for that."

"How?" Hugo asked, snapping at him. "By crushing my spirit? By making me feel like nothing I ever did was good enough? You never even tried to understand me. Not once. You just decided who you thought I should be and then punished me when I was not that person."

Heinrich's gaze darkened, a hint of the man he once was emerging from the recesses of his soul. "And what was I supposed to understand, Hugo? That you were different? That you needed... what exactly? Kindness? Coddling? Life doesn't offer those things. It was only a moment ago that you told me you did not even understand yourself. How can you, in good faith, expect the world to understand a thing like you when that thing does not even have the slightest idea of its own nature?"

Heinrich rose to his feet, his frail frame quivering with the effort. For a moment, he appeared to grow taller, the force of his fury invigorating him. Hugo flinched; his own pent-up indignation stifled for a moment, as if he might choke on his own tongue.

"You want to talk, my boy?" Heinrich went on, his voice

escalating with each passing syllable. "Let's talk. I see you. You think I don't? You think yourself invisible to the world—that you lie beyond its reach; that you're better than it all—but the fact of the matter is, reality eludes you. I can see you clear as day; the frightened child, the weak-willed soul—I can see it all. So, trust me when I tell you I can sure as hell see the empty shadow standing before me. You are not invisible, son. You're just not as compelling as you think you are."

Caught in the tempest of his emotions, Hugo didn't say a word. Here lay the confrontation he had long been yearning for, yet now that it had arrived, brought on by his own words and actions, he seemed to want no part in it. Filled with angst, he unconsciously fiddled with his hands, drawing his father's eye.

"Everything I ever did was for you both, Hugo. I wanted you to be strong, to survive in this world. How did you repay me? By running off and stealing from me." He gestured sharply towards Hugo's hand. "That ring you're wearing—it was not yours to take."

"It was to be mine."

"You stole it," Heinrich said. "I would have passed it down to you, but you stole it before you earned it."

"I didn't think you'd notice," Hugo lied.

"Of course I noticed. It is more than just a piece of jewellery, Hugo. It embodies a legacy."

Hugo's entire body ached, the weight of the ring becoming unbearable. "A legacy of what? Control? Cruelty? I did not really want it. Still, I do not. I took it because it was the only thing that felt like it belonged to me."

Heinrich's eyes softened, though his demeanour remained guarded. "Despite your assertions, you are as guilty of misunderstanding as any of us. That ring is not about control. It's about responsibility. About carrying something forward, even when it feels impossible."

"Responsibility?" Hugo forced a bitter laugh, his hands shaking. "You mean like how you carried us forward? How you carried her forward, right into the grave?"

The words hit Heinrich like a slap, and his face crumpled. Moments later, the words had knocked him off his feet, rendering him utterly undone, and he slumped back into his armchair once more. "I failed her," he said, his voice barely audible. "I did. And I failed you."

Hugo halted, the admission slicing through his simmering anger like a blade through flesh. He had longed for this moment, for as long as he could remember. He had wanted to hear his father acknowledge—however minutely—the scars that he had inflicted. But now, as those very words hung in the air, they brought him no relief. Despite a momentary rise to passion, Hugo knew that this was not the same man who had left indelible marks on his soul. If his words were to be deemed a currency, then their value had plummeted.

"You were supposed to protect us," Hugo said, still pushing for something more to come of the confrontation. "But all you ever did was demand obedience."

"I was teaching you strength."

"All you taught me was resentment... and how to leave."

"You think I lacked affection for you? I loved you the only way I knew how. I stayed. I provided. I sacrificed. And you threw it all back in my face."

Hugo regarded him, his anger now gone, replaced by something much colder. "Love is not staying. It is trying. It is understanding. And you never tried. You broke everything you touched, including her."

"Do you think I am unaware of that? She was the only thing I ever got right... for a while. Now she is lost to me."

"And what of me? Was I just a mistake?"

"No. But I made you think you were."

Hugo turned away, his throat tight and his chest now hollow. He had wanted this for so long, but now, standing in the ruins of his father's life, he felt nothing but emptiness.

With heavy, unsteady steps, he approached the door. As he reached the exit, his father's voice stopped him.

"I stayed for her," Heinrich whispered. "But I could not save her. Just like I could not save you. I see now... that her funeral was for you both."

Hugo didn't respond. He withdrew into the dim corridor, the sound of the crackling fire receding into the distance as he walked back to his room. The burden of exchanged words—and those left unuttered—swirled in his mind. His hands felt heavy at his sides, the ring on his finger colder than ever. He had hoped for resolution, but what he'd unearthed was an emptiness greater than he had been prepared for, one he knew he'd never fill.

He sank onto the bed, the weary mattress crying beneath him. Curled into himself, his body quaked with a mixture of anger, sorrow, and exhaustion. He stared up at the cracked ceiling, his thoughts unravelling like threads pulled from a frayed tapestry of memories.

The fire in his chest burned out, leaving only ash.

CHAPTER TWENTY-THREE
Contacts

The carriage juddered along the uneven road, wheels grinding against cobblestones. Hugo sat in the back, his body jolting with every rut and dip, though he registered little of it. He fixed his eyes on the small window, but he didn't perceive the passing scenery—a blur of indistinct and lifeless grey and brown. Autumn was in its final throes, clinging to what insignificant life remained before winter would soon come to consume the rest of it.

The sky hung low, a flat expanse of slate that promised neither warmth nor reprieve. Berlin would soon be behind him, though its weight would crush his chest for a long time to come.

The house had been hushed that morning when he left. No servants saw him off; he had told them not to bother. His father hadn't appeared either, though Hugo hadn't expected him to. He had slipped out as quietly as he had the first time, his ghostly footsteps echoing in the hollow corridors.

He leaned back in the carriage, resting his head against the worn leather. The air inside was cold, laced with the faintest scent of horses and damp earth. The coachman's murmurs to someone ahead drifted back to him, incomprehensible but hypnotically rhythmic. Hugo closed his eyes, letting the sounds outside wash over him.

We avoided each other in the end, he thought. *Fitting.*

In the days following their confrontation, the house had settled into an uneasy quietness. Heinrich kept to his study, shutting himself away behind the heavy oak door. Hugo, unwilling to cross that boundary again, roamed the house like a ghost. His presence felt but never acknowledged.

On one of those aimless afternoons, the servant approached him. She carried a leather-bound notebook, its edges worn, the spine cracked from years of use.

"This is for you, Master Henke," she said, holding it out to him.

Hugo took it, his brow furrowing as he turned it over in his hands. Neat handwriting filled the pages, with names and addresses organised by country and city. Many were in Germany, but there were others—France, Belgium, Switzerland. And then, towards the back, a section labelled Great Britain.

"What's this?" he asked, though he already had an inkling.

"It's your father's book of contacts. He thought... he thought it might help you."

Hugo's grip on the book tightened. "He told you to bring this to me?"

"Yes," she said. "He... wouldn't give it to you himself."

Of course he wouldn't. His pride wouldn't allow it. Even in this slight gesture, Heinrich had maintained his distance, able to avoid any direct acknowledgement of what they had discussed in his study.

Hugo flipped through the pages, his eyes scanning the near rows of names. One caught his attention—Frederick Ansell, a name he recognised from conversation overheard in years past. Ansell was a German-born editor who had established himself at a reputable newspaper in London.

Later that same evening, Hugo sat down and wrote a letter to Ansell, explaining his situation with careful diplomacy. He mentioned his father, though he framed the connection as nothing more than a passing courtesy. He included a copy of his academic credentials, carefully tucked into the envelope.

The reply came much faster than Hugo had expected.

Ansell's tone was polite but brisk, offering Hugo an interview upon his return to London. It wasn't a job offer, but it was a start. When the servant delivered the letter to him, she had smiled, as though she understood its significance. "I'm glad, Master Henke," she had said.

Berlin rolled past the carriage windows, its muted colours blending into one another. The house had long since faded into the distance, but it had not left Hugo's thoughts. He kept thinking of its corridors, cold and silent, and of its garden, overgrown and wild. He thought of the fire in the hearth, its embers collapsing inward, just like his father.

In the days prior to his departure, the silence between them had grown almost unbearable. Hugo had regularly imagined his father seeking him out, perhaps to offer some last words, but none came. Instead, he heard only the faint sound of papers rustling behind the closed study door, a sound that had become as much a part of the house as the creaking of the floorboards.

I guess this is it, Hugo thought. *Goodbye, Father.*

He closed his eyes, the image of his mother's grave flashing unbidden in his mind. The wound in the earth, refusing to heal. The words he had spoken that day felt so distant now, half-formed things that hadn't come close to touching the depth of what he had wanted to say.

In the darkness of his mind, as the carriage continued to rattle along, he saw her face. Her expression was a mixture of pride and sadness. He could hear her distant voice, the words from her letter echoing in his memory.

You have always been more than he sees in you, Hugo. I hope you see it too.

Her words, well-meaning as they had been, were hollow. Nothing could ever change that.

When Hugo's train arrived in London, the sun had almost set, casting long shadows across the platform. Hugo stepped out, his legs almost as stiff as his soul from the journey, and he wrapped his coat around him. He felt no sense of homecoming as London loomed ahead of him, only a flicker of dread.

He began walking, his steps slow and deliberate. The city rose around him, its buildings turning dark against the transitioning sky. Somewhere, a clock chimed, its sound distant and hollow.

He didn't know what lay ahead of him, and for the first time in his life, he didn't care. The only thing he was sure of was that the city would swallow him again. Just as it always had.

PART 3

WINTER

A Dream of Bones

CHAPTER TWENTY-FOUR
Afloat

The office hummed with life, its walls alive with voices that rose and fell like the rhythms of a crowded marketplace. Desks stretched across the room in neat rows, their surfaces cluttered with stacks of papers, ink-stained blotters, and the occasional cup of lukewarm tea or coffee. Clerks darted between them, carrying proofs and manuscripts, the clatter of their footsteps echoing in the bustling newsroom, while editors barked instructions to reporters, their voices sharp and urgent, who scribbled furiously in notebooks, pencils scratching against paper. The sharp, almost metallic tang of fresh ink mingled with the smooth, woody aroma of varnished wood, creating an atmosphere of industry and purpose.

Hugo sat at his desk near the window, the clamour swirling around him like a storm, a muted roar that barely touched him. The wind howled faintly, rattling the windowpanes beside him, offering a view of the grey, windswept sky and a distant, lonely church spire. A weak, pallid light filtered through, casting long shadows that stretched and shifted across the room.

He stared at the blank sheet of paper in front of him, his pen hovering above it. The article was due by the end of the day—a commentary on some parliamentary debate or other. Though he'd attended the session, listened intently, and meticulously recorded notes, the details were now a hazy fog in his mind.

A sigh escaped his lips as he dipped his pen in the inkpot and commenced writing; the words flowed mechanically from his pen. As always, his sentences were clear, concise, and compelling—everything they needed to be—but to him, they felt hollow, as though they belonged to someone else.

The job was a far cry from the monotonous translation work he had been doing before. This was a reputable newspaper, its name whispered with respect in the circles of power and influence. The editors demanded excellence, and Hugo delivered it. He had penned articles on everything from the chaos of labour strikes, vividly describing picket lines and impassioned speeches, to the complexities of foreign policy, offering insightful analyses of international relations; his work consistently praised for its clarity and incisive perspective.

But the praise, ringing hollow in his ears, meant nothing to him.

He wrote, each word a heavy, grey brick adding to the wall, a soundless construction of his retreat from a world that had become a cacophony of noise and meaninglessness. The office, for all its warmth and energy, felt as lifeless to him as some ancient crypt. To Hugo, the warmth was artificial, a trick of the gas lamps and bustling bodies. The voices he heard were always distant, a symphony played for deaf ears.

A shadow fell across his desk, pulling him from his thoughts. He looked up to see a colleague whose name he had never bothered to learn—a man in his early thirties with a ruddy complexion and a perpetually cheerful demeanour. Just a short while ago, Hugo would have despised such a man—the mere sight of him churning his stomach—now, though, he felt only a cold apathy.

"Henke," the man said, his voice carrying the dreaded lilt of camaraderie. "You're always so damn quiet. What are you working on?"

"An article," Hugo said curtly, keeping his eyes on the page.

Undeterred by Hugo's icy response, the man let out a hearty laugh, the sound bouncing off the nearby walls. "Well, I could've guessed that much. What's it about?"

Hugo set down his pen, meeting the man's gaze for the first time. "Politics," he said flatly. "Parliamentary debates. The usual."

"Well, it's good work you're doing," the man said with a grin. "You should celebrate sometime. Come out with us tonight. We're heading to The Blue Lion after hours. First round's on me."

Hugo hesitated, his mind racing through a litany of excuses. "I appreciate the offer, but I have some things to take care of at home."

Furrowing his brow, the man gave a slow, almost reluctant nod. "Fair enough, Henke. But don't be a stranger, yeah? It wouldn't kill you to loosen up now and then."

Hugo offered a faint smile that didn't reach his eyes. "Work is only good if it matters. And it doesn't."

The man opened his mouth to respond, a string of words forming on his lips, then he thought better of it. He clapped Hugo on the shoulder and walked away, leaving Hugo alone once more with his blank page.

As the afternoon wore on, the office grew louder, the atmosphere thick with the sound of typewriters and murmured conversations. Hugo worked in silence—as he always did—his pen scratching against the paper as he forced himself to focus. The words came easy—too easy, as though they had been waiting for him all along.

When he finished, he set down his pen and leaned back in his chair, staring at the ceiling for a while. The gas lamps above flickered, their light casting uneven patterns across the room. For a moment, he closed his eyes, letting the din of the office wash over him.

He thought of Berlin, of the hollow house he had left behind. He thought of his father, hunched in his chair, and his mother's letter, still folded neatly in his drawer at home. Of course, he thought of Emily, her face a ghost in his memory, forever present in the garden where they had met.

What's the point in any of this? he wondered. Though not new, the thought's icy tendrils wrapped around him, lingering longer than usual, a stiff wind whispering doubts in his ear.

By the time the office had emptied out, Hugo was still at his desk, his article completed and handed in. The others had left in small groups, their laughter echoing and fading as the last of them disappeared into the evening.

Hugo remained seated for some time, the only sound the gentle hum of the city as he stared out the window at the darkened street below. Snow had begun to fall, each flake catching the gaslight's glow before drifting to the ground, creating a soft hush. The city seemed quieter now, as though the snow had muffled its usual chaos.

With a sigh, he finally stood, the rough wool of his coat scratching against his skin as he pulled it on and adjusted his worn hat. He extinguished the lamp on his desk, plunging his corner of the office into darkness. As he made his way to the door, his footsteps echoed against the wooden floor, a solitary sound in the empty room.

Outside, the air bit at his exposed skin, the sharp, stiff wind whipping around him as the snow crunched with each step. The streets were almost empty, save for the occasional figure that hurried past, their heads bowed against the wind.

Hugo buried his hands deep in his pockets, his breath puffing out in white clouds. He walked without direction, as he often did as of late, letting the city carry him wherever it pleased. The snow continued to fall, erasing the sharp edges of the world around him.

As he passed a small cafe, the warm light spilling from its windows caught his attention. He paused for a bit, watching the people inside as they laughed and gestured, their faces lit with a warmth he'd never know.

They have something special, he thought. *And they don't even know it.*

Hugo turned away, his footsteps carrying him through the evening, into the night.

CHAPTER TWENTY-FIVE
Shards of Silence

He was walking, though he couldn't remember where he had started walking from. The snow beneath his feet was thick and undisturbed, crunching as with each step. Around him stretched an endless forest, the trees towering impossibly high, their blackened trunks rough to the touch, and their branches interwoven above like a web, choking out the sky. A strange, flat light, devoid of a source, illuminated the world, casting no shadows, and making everything seem muted and unreal.

Heavy, cold air pressed against him, though he could not see his breath. Each step seemed weightier than the one before, the snow clinging to his boots like a shroud, as if the very forest conspired to hold him back. The oppressive silence was deafening; a vacuum of sound that filled his ears with the phantom ringing of nothingness. For a moment, he considered if this overwhelming numbness—this chilling stillness—might be what death felt like.

Somewhere far off, laughter broke through the stillness. A woman's voice, soft and lilting, though its sweetness carried an edge that made Hugo's stomach churn.

Emily.

He froze in place, his heart leaping in his chest. The sound came again, echoing through the trees, ricocheting between the trunks. Its origin was indeterminate, yet Hugo reacted at once, his body moving before his mind could object.

"Emily," he called, though his voice came out muted, snatched from him by the surrounding air. He tried again, louder this time, but the result was the same. The sound seemed to die the moment it left his lips.

The laughter grew louder, closer, weaving through the trees like a taunt. He quickened his pace, his breaths coming in sharp bursts, though somehow, the freezing air did not sting his lungs.

"Emily!"

As he ran, the trees seemed to lean closer, their gnarled branches scraping against his clothes, like skeletal claws reaching for him. The snow deepened, pulling at his legs, but he pushed forward, determined, the laughter guiding him. It grew sharper, more fragmented, splintering into a chorus of voices. His mother. His father. A child.

The sound wrapped around him, suffocating, unbearable. He stumbled, falling to his knees, the snow soaking through his trousers. The laughter ceased.

Hugo looked up.

Before him was a frozen lake, the ice clouded and opaque, muffling any sound of water and reflecting the grey sky. The forest stopped abruptly at the water's edge, the dark trunks forming an ominous, jagged wall behind him. The lake stretched out forever, disappearing into the grey horizon.

He rose to his feet, trembling as he stepped closer to the edge. A faint shimmer emanated from the ice, its surface disrupted by veins of black that pulsed with a soft, almost imperceptible rhythm. Beneath the ice, shadows began to stir.

At first, they appeared as shapeless, amorphous forms, swirling and shifting like ink dropped into water, a mesmerising, dark ballet. But as Hugo watched them, they began to take shape.

First came his mother's face, its features stark and angular against the dim light, her gaze unfocused and distant. Her lips moved, but no sound came. Her eyes locked onto his, and for a moment, he thought he saw tears glistening there.

Behind her, another figure emerged. His father, rigid and imposing, his face a mask of disapproval. His lips were moving too, his words silent, but furious.

More figures joined them. Emily, her hair spilling over her shoulders, her eyes filled with something Hugo hadn't seen from her before, something he couldn't place—pity, perhaps, or regret. And then, finally, a young boy.

The boy was no more than seven or eight, his face pale and pinched with fear. He clutched a small, smooth wooden toy, its paint chipped and worn, his eyes darting around, searching for something or someone.

Hugo's chest tightened, his breath coming in shallow gasps. The boy looked up at him, their gazes locking. The toy fell from the boy's hands, landing on the ice with a soulless thud.

Hugo knelt at the edge of the lake, his hands pressing against its frozen surface. It was colder than anything he had ever felt, and the chill seeped through his skin, into his bones.

"Wait," his voice trembled. "Don't go."

The figures ignored him, drifting further beneath the ice. Hugo's panic surged, a frantic, desperate energy that made him pound against the unyielding surface with his fists, his knuckles white.

"Don't leave!" he screamed, his voice breaking. "I'm here! I'm right here!"

The ice refused to break. He struck it again, harder this time, a sharp, agonising pain exploding through his hands. The figures continued to fade, their outlines becoming a blur once more.

He scrambled to his feet, searching for something, for anything, to break the ice. He found a jagged rock half-buried in the snow. With numb and clumsy fingers, he seized it, the icy chill seeping into him. He swung it with a mighty heave, sending it crashing against the glassy surface of the lake, the shock reverberating through his arms.

The ice did not crack.

Desperation clawed at his chest. He struck it again, and again. Each time, the rock rebounded, the ice seeming to grow thicker with each strike.

"Please," he whined, tears streaming down his face. "Please."

His arms gave out, the rock slipping from his hands. He collapsed onto the ice, his body trembling with exhaustion and despair.

He stared down at the surface, his breath now fogging the glassy expanse. The shadows were gone, swallowed by the darkness beneath. All that remained was his own reflection, staring back at him.

But it wasn't quite right.

The reflection's eyes were sharper, piercing like shards of glass, its expression a frozen mask of disdain. It tilted its head, as though studying him. And then, slowly, it began to smile.

At first, just a flicker of a smile, almost invisible, then it spread, stretching impossibly wide, a grotesque parody of mirth. The reflection's teeth gleamed white against the darkness, and its eyes burned with something cruel and knowing.

Hugo tried to look away, but the horrifying sight captivated him, his body frozen in fear.

The reflection's lips moved, a silent whisper lost to the glacial chill, and then it began to fade, dissolving into the ice with a final, brittle crack, leaving only his own desolate reflection.

Hugo lay there, his face pressed against the frozen lake, the cold numbing him completely. He wanted to scream, but his voice had abandoned him.

Hugo woke with a heaving chest, his breath caught somewhere between a gasp and a choke, his dream lingering like frost on his skin. His body felt damp, his clothes clinging to his skin as though the cold from his dream had seeped through the walls of sleep.

For a moment, he couldn't quite place where he was. The walls of his small flat were indistinct in the predawn light. The glass muted the faint hum of the city beyond the window, as though it, too, were distant and dreamlike.

He sat up, his head swimming with the remnants of the nightmare. His hands, stiff and aching, trembled as he rubbed them together, seeking warmth but finding only the lingering cold; the feeling was precisely that of having struck that unyielding ice.

Without thinking, he swung his legs over the side of the bed, his feet hitting the worn wooden floor with a soft thud, and stood. His movements were mechanical, driven by an impulse he couldn't explain. He crossed the room to the window, pulling back the curtain.

A cloak of frost covered the city, and snow blanketed its streets. Buildings stood silent and dark, their edges softened by the night. It was still too early for most to be awake; the city caught in that strange liminal space between night and dawn.

The outside chill summoned him, its keenness offering lucidity despite its cruelty.

CHAPTER TWENTY-SIX
Treading the Abyss

The city, under a heavy blanket of snow, appeared more like another of Hugo's dreams than reality. Layers of frost and ice smothered the city's typical sounds—as if the snow had stolen its voice.

Hugo moved through the streets like a ghost, the wind's bite and the weight of the clinging snow unfelt on his shoulders. In the city's quiet, peace reigned—softened, distant, untouched by the chaos of life—as though mirroring Hugo's own state of mind.

He turned onto a familiar street, his footsteps faltering as the wrought-iron gate of the garden came into view. The snow lay thick upon the pathways, concealing the spots where he and Emily had once stood. The bench where they had once sat was now just a white mound, its edges softened and indistinct.

Hugo paused at the gate, his hand resting on the cold metal. The frost burned against his skin, but he didn't pull away. He stared through the cold, unforgiving bars, his chest tightening with each painful memory that surfaced.

Go inside, he thought. *Just once more.*

But an unseen force held his feet rooted to the spot. The garden felt like a sanctuary for someone else now, a place that had belonged to another version of himself—one who had still believed in connection, in the possibility of being understood. That version of him was gone—if he had ever even existed—buried beneath the snow along with everything else.

He let his hand fall from the gate, and then he turned away.

The apartment building where Emily had lived wasn't far. He hadn't intended to go, yet his steps led him there anyway. The streets grew narrower as he walked, the buildings on either side looming tall and dark, their windows shuttered and lifeless.

He stopped opposite the building, staring up at the second-floor window, the one that had belonged to her. The shutters were closed, the sill thick with snow. All signs of life were absent; it appeared nobody had ever inhabited the place.

For a moment, he imagined climbing the steps, knocking on the door, and finding her there. She would open it, her hair dishevelled, her face lit with joyous surprise. She would invite him in, her voice warm and familiar, and they would sit together by the window, watching the snow fall as if no time had passed at all.

But the longer he stared at the lifeless building, the more the fantasy unravelled—the shutters remained closed, and the door shunned him. His hopeful warmth dissolved into the cold reality. Emily was gone, as distant and unreachable as the sky buried behind the thick winter clouds. Hands shoved deep in his pockets, Hugo turned and walked away.

By the time he reached the Thames, the first light of dawn was creeping over the horizon, painting the eastern sky with soft hues of pink and orange. The river crawled, a sluggish, dark serpent, its surface impenetrable except for the occasional glittering shard of ice.

Hugo stood on the embankment, the cold stone railing pressing into his hands. The water seemed to hold all the weight of the world, carrying it downstream without hesitation or complaint. He imagined it carrying away his regrets, the moments he wished he could undo, the words he had left unsaid. He tried with all his might, but the weight on his chest would not lift.

It's not enough, he thought. *It's never enough.*

Cleansing and destructive, the river presented a paradox. A graveyard for the past, and a cradle for the future. He wondered just how many others had stood there before him, gazing into the same dark waters, their hearts just as heavy.

Hugo found a snow-covered bench near the river's edge; he brushed the snow off with his coat sleeve before sitting down, feeling the cold seep through his trousers. He bent forward, resting his elbows on his knees, his breath puffing out in the frigid air.

Sounds of the awakening city—a distant cart, a muffled dog bark—broke the silence. But the snow still held its dominion, muting the sharp edges of the world. He watched it continue to fall, each flake drifting lazily to the ground. It covered everything, without bias, hiding imperfections and beauty equally beneath a layer of cold indifference.

It erases everything, Hugo thought. *Not permanently, but long enough to make you forget what lies beneath.*

He decided that the snow was a metaphor, a soft numb blanket over the jaggedness of life. It didn't heal or fix anything, but it made the sharp edges bearable, at least for a while.

For the first time in what felt like hours, he let his shoulders slump, and the tension drain from his body. Reclined on the bench, he tilted his head towards the sky. Watching the growing light that painted the clouds with soft colours, for a moment, he felt something close to peace.

Not happiness, not hope—those were things he no longer sought. But a stillness pervaded him, a brief acceptance of the emptiness he carried.

CHAPTER TWENTY-SEVEN
Nothing Left to Hold

The newsroom emptied, voices rising in casual chatter as the reporters and clerks gathered their belongings and buttoned up their coats. The sound of chairs scraping against the floor mingled with the rustling of papers and the click of typewriters being covered for the night.

Hugo sat at his desk, a half-written article beside his resting hand. An hour had gone by, and he hadn't touched it—his thoughts were elsewhere. Around him, the air buzzed with the energy of people eager to leave work behind, their laughter spilling out into the room as a reminder of something he'd never been part of.

"Henke!" a voice called, cutting through the noise. Hugo looked up to see his colleague—the same ruddy-faced man who had tried to engage him before—standing by the door, his hat already in hand. "We're heading to The Blue Lion for a drink. You coming this time?"

A flicker of hesitation crossed Hugo's face as his eyes darted to the people gathered at the exit. Their grins, bright with expectation, hinted that the promise of warmth and alcohol would erase the day's tiredness. "I'll pass," he said, his voice low, but firm.

The man shrugged. "Suit yourself. But one of these days, Henke, you're going to have to learn how to have a bit of fun."

Hugo did not respond, and the group soon disappeared from the office, their laughter fading into the evening. The room appeared larger now, the echo of their departure lingering in the air.

He sat for a while, staring at the blank spaces between his notes, the silence amplifying the thoughts in his head. A nameless anxiety washed over him at the thought of returning to the dim, musty confines of his flat. The brandy bottle on his shelf was empty, and the idea of sitting in that small, silent room without a drink seemed unbearable.

At last, he rose, collecting his coat and scarf. If he needed a drink, he could readily find one somewhere else.

He picked a pub that was a long way from The Blue Lion. A side street he had stumbled upon by chance tucked it away, its wooden sign groaning in the wind. The light that spilled from its windows was dim and yellow, the kind that promised a quiet corner rather than a lively crowd.

Inside, the air was thick with the smell of ale and smoke. The small room, panelled in dark wood, held a handful of patrons scattered across mismatched tables and stools. A fire burned low in the hearth, its glow failing to reach the far corners of the room.

Approaching the bar, Hugo sat down at the far end. The bartender, a middle-aged man with tired eyes, nodded at him without a word and poured him a brandy. Though Hugo wondered how the man could have known he favoured brandy, he was not concerned enough to inquire. He took a sip; the warmth spread through his chest with an almost medicinal effect.

"You look like you've had a long day," a voice said, pulling Hugo's attention to the man seated two stools down.

He was an older man, perhaps in his sixties, his face a roadmap of wrinkles etched by years of hard living. Frayed edges marked his coat, and the cold had reddened his knuckles. An almost empty pint sat in front of him, the rim of the glass smudged.

"I suppose I have," Hugo said.

The man chuckled, the sound like gravel grinding together.

"Haven't we all?" He took a long drink of his dregs, then set the glass down with a heavy sigh. "You work nearby?"

Hugo nodded, but didn't elaborate.

The man squinted at him, as if trying to read something in his expression. "What's your line of work?"

"Writing."

"Ah, a writer. Got to be clever for that. Always wanted to try my hand at it, but don't reckon I've got the patience. Or the wit."

Saying nothing, Hugo took another sip of brandy.

The man seemed content to fill the silence with himself. "I was a carpenter, you know. Built things with my hands. It's honest work, but it takes its toll." He held up his hands, the knuckles swollen and gnarled. "Not much use for these anymore."

Hugo glanced at the man's calloused hands, noticing the dirt ingrained under his fingernails, but didn't respond.

The man forced another chuckle. "Ah, listen to me, rambling on. My wife used to say I could talk the ears off a mule." His smile faltered, the weight of something unspoken settling over him. "She's gone now. Passed five years back. Took the best parts of me with her."

Hugo stared into his drink, swirling the liquid in the glass. The man's words were the kind he'd heard before—lamentations of loss and regret—but they struck a chord he couldn't easily ignore.

"Lost a son too. War took him. Or maybe it was the waiting after. Hard to say." He paused, staring into his empty glass. "The world takes what it wants, son. It doesn't ask. It doesn't care."

As the words hit him, Hugo's grip on his glass tightened, his chest constricted.

"You learn not to hold on too tightly," the man said, his gaze drifting.

Hugo swallowed the last of his brandy, the burn doing little to ease the tightness in his throat. "There's nothing left to hold," he said, finally engaging, though he spoke more to himself than to the man.

The man turned to look at him, his eyes clouded with something between pity and understanding. A moment of silence stretched between them, fragile as a thread.

The bartender approached, refilling the man's pint without a word. He raised it with a slight, fatigued movement before taking a sip.

"Well," he said after a moment, his tone lighter now, but no less hollow, "enough of my blabbing. You take care of yourself. This world's hard enough without us making it worse for each other."

Hugo nodded, his gaze fixed on the bar.

The man downed his pint and then stood, his steps slow and uneven as he made his way to the door. The sound of it closing behind him left the room quieter than it had been before.

Hugo sat for a while longer, his empty glass in front of him, the fire in the hearth dying down, as if it, too, were running out of reasons to keep going. The bartender glanced his way, gaze questioning, and without a word, Hugo tapped the rim of his glass with his finger. The brandy came at once, filling the void in front of him, its amber warmth promising the briefest reprieve. He stared into it, sensing the pull of its depth, knowing it wouldn't be his last tonight.

CHAPTER TWENTY-EIGHT
The Woman in Red

The pub door closed behind him with a hollow thud, the sound lingering in his ears as he walked. Before him, the city extended, a concrete maze under a sky void of stars; the night felt heavy, oppressive, and utterly endless.

Rounding a corner, he noticed the dim light of a gas lamp highlighting a figure outside another nearby pub. A woman, cloaked in red, stood there; her coat was vivid against the monochrome world of snow and shadow. A cigarette dangled from her fingers, the ember flared as she brought it to her lips.

Hugo stopped dead in his tracks, his breath catching in his throat.

Emily.

His heart jolted, a sharp, almost painful sensation breaking through the fog of alcohol and apathy. His eyes fixated on her, a million thoughts battling in his mind as he struggled to accept what his eyes were telling him. She was here, as though the universe had decided, in a rare act of mercy, to return her to him.

His steps faltered forward—slow and hesitant—a nervous tremor in his legs, as if afraid the moment would shatter if he moved too fast. His thoughts spiralled as he grasped at the threads of a fantasy he didn't dare believe.

He imagined her turning towards him; her face lighting up

with that soft, knowing smile that had once made him feel understood. She would call his name, a soft, warm sound that held a hint of surprise.

"Hugo," she would say, as though the name itself had been waiting on her tongue for many nights.

And he would answer, a torrent of regret and longing pouring from his lips, each word tumbling over the next. He would tell her everything—the things he hadn't said in her home, the truths he had buried beneath layers of fear and pride.

"I've been a fool," he would confess. "I didn't know how to hold on. But I see it now. I see you."

And she would forgive him, her hand reaching for his, the warmth of her touch grounding him in a way he had never known. Together, they would step into the warmth of the pub, into a world where second chances were not just a cruel fiction.

The fantasy unfurled in vivid detail, so real he could almost hear her voice, almost feel the warmth of her touch. A sensation, dormant for weeks, maybe months, began to rouse within him; a tiny spark, like a fragile ember fighting against the encroaching darkness.

But as he drew closer, the dream unravelled.

Her posture, so casual and unhurried, did not match Emily's movements, which had always been awkward, laced with a nervous energy. Her hair, caught in the lamplight, lacked Emily's distinct sheen.

And then she turned.

The cigarette glowed between her fingers, her lips pursed as she exhaled a thin stream of smoke. Her honest face, sharp and angular, was not at all familiar. No—Hugo realised with a sinking certainty—it wasn't unfamiliar. It was her.

The woman from months ago. From back in the summer. Her red coat, so vivid against the city's dull backdrop, was the one he'd spied on the street that morning. The one who had taken up space with a confidence he had both envied and hated. The one who he had first mistaken Emily for in the garden.

She stood beneath the gas lamp now, just as she had then, her expression unreadable as she glanced at him. She caught his eye, her gaze lingering for only a moment before she turned her attention back to the cigarette in her hand.

A few steps away, Hugo stopped, his heart plummeting back into the familiar numbness. The brief flare of the ember inside him died, leaving only the faintest trace of ash.

It wasn't Emily. Of course, it wasn't Emily.

The woman noticed him approaching before he had stopped, her head tilted, cigarette poised between her fingers, and the smoke curling in the cold air. Her red coat seemed even brighter up close.

"Evening," she said, her voice tinged with an amused warmth. Her gaze was sharp, but not unkind, her dark eyes narrowing as they swept over him. "You've got the look of a man who carries the weight of the world."

Though it held no sincerity, he gave her a faint smile, the lamplight casting faint shadows across his face. "Not the world. Just myself."

She took a drag of her cigarette, her lips curving into a small, intrigued smile as she exhaled. "Maybe you should put it down."

"There's no one to hand it to," he said, his tone devoid of self-pity, but heavy with resignation.

She studied him for a moment, her head dipping, as if weighing his words. Then she laughed, a low, throaty sound that seemed more lived-in than joyous. "That's a shame," she said, flicking ash from the cigarette onto the ground. "You look like a man who could use the relief."

Hugo didn't respond, his eyes shifting from the faint wisp of smoke rising from her hand. Her scent reached him—something floral and warm, mingling with the acrid tang of tobacco. Though pleasant, perhaps even alluring, he dismissed it with a thought that burned like acid. She wasn't *her*.

Down the street from the pub, they found a bench; a layer of snow dusted the wooden slats. The woman wiped it clean with her gloved hand before sitting, her movements deliberate, but unsteady, her intoxication betraying itself in the way she leaned against the armrest.

Hugo hesitated before taking a seat beside her, his hands buried in his pockets. The cold seeped through his coat, but he ignored it, his attention drawn to the way the light played across the woman's features.

She was beautiful—her sharp cheekbones, the curve of her lips, the faint flush on her cheeks from the cold. But it didn't matter. No matter how perfectly she fit the image of beauty, she wasn't *her*.

"So," said the woman, breaking the silence, "what's a brooding man like you doing out in the cold tonight?"

"I could ask you the same thing."

She smiled, nodding her head to acknowledge his fair point. "I needed some air," she said, lifting her cigarette to her lips again. "Too much noise inside. Too many people pretending to be happy."

Hugo huffed a quiet laugh, more breath than sound. "It seems to be the season for it," he said with a dry amusement.

A softening expression accompanied the woman's assessing glance. "And you? What are you running from?"

His gaze drifted to the snow-covered street in front of them. "Nothing," he said after a long pause. "There's nothing left to run from."

She scrutinised him for a moment, her brow furrowing. "That's the saddest thing I've ever heard."

Silence settled between them, punctuated only by the rhythmic crackle of her cigarette.

"What do you desire?" she asked, the insistence in her voice leaving no room for refusal.

"Desire?"

She nodded, her dark eyes locking onto his. "Yes. Everyone wants something, even if they pretend like they don't. So, what is it you want?"

He hesitated, the alcohol's effect a subtle loosening of his inhibitions, but the deepest truths stayed locked inside. "I'm not sure."

She leaned closer, her breath ghosting over his cheek as her gaze remained unwavering. "No one's ever not sure. Come on. Indulge me."

Hugo exhaled, trying to survive under the weight of her attention—the way her words pressed against him like a dare. Finally, he spoke, his voice low and unsteady, the words tumbling out before he could stop them. "I'd give everything... everything I have... everything. I'd give it all back. To be loved for one night."

The woman's eyes widened, and the cigarette hanging forgotten between her fingers almost slipped free. She straightened in her seat, her expression unreadable to him. Then a slow, deliberate smile spread across her face, crinkling the corners of her eyes.

"Let me love you," she said, her voice barely above a whisper. "Just for tonight."

His breath hitched, the words assaulting him. For a fleeting moment, he imagined what it would be like to say yes—to let her warmth fill the void inside him; to surrender to something... anything that might make him feel less empty.

But the thought dissolved as quickly as it had come. She wasn't *her*, she never could be *her*. She would never understand him.

"No." Hugo shook his head.

Her smile trembled, replaced by a puzzled frown as confusion etched itself into her features. "Why not?"

"Because you don't understand. You can't. Even if you could... you are not the one. You are too real."

The words hung in the air between them, heavy and irrevocable. The woman stared at him, her expression shifting from confusion to something else—perhaps pity, or maybe even frustration. She turned away, taking a long drag from her cigarette before exhaling a burst of smoke.

"You're a strange one, aren't you?" she said, her tone attempting levity, but failing. "I don't think I've ever met anyone quite like you."

Hugo didn't respond. He didn't care to. He just stared at the snow gathering on the street, his thoughts a tangled mess of regret and resignation.

The woman stubbed out her cigarette against the bench, unsteady as she rose to her feet. "Well," she said, brushing the ash from her gloves, "I hope you figure it out. Whatever it is you're looking for."

He looked up at her, his eyes burdened with something

unspoken. "I'm not looking for anything."

She hesitated, as though considering her next words, but then she shook her head and turned away, her red coat disappearing up the street and back inside the warm pub.

Hugo remained on the bench, the cold seeping into his bones as the silence of the night closed in around him once more.

CHAPTER TWENTY-NINE
A Symphony in White

Hugo walked, though the act felt more like sinking. The ground, invisible beneath the fog, seemed to clutch at his boots with each step he took, holding him back, testing his resolve. The air was thick and oppressive, damp and cold, coiling around his chest like a vice.

Nothing broke the monotony of the fog—an infinite sea of grey and white, neither light, nor dark, with no sound to be heard but that of Hugo's own breath. He didn't know how long he had been walking, nor why he continued. No guidance existed; no points of reference. Only the unrelenting fog, swallowing everything—including him.

And then, somewhere ahead, something broke through. Barely perceptible at first, a trembling pinprick of light flickered; it could have very well been his imagination. But as he moved towards it, it grew stronger, cutting through the murky expanse like a solitary star. The light didn't just beckon him—it demanded his attention, pulsing as though it shared a heartbeat with the fog itself.

Hugo's feet carried him forward, unsure if curiosity or compulsion guided him. The light grew brighter, shifting and undulating like a flame caught in an invisible wind. It emitted no warmth, only a cold radiance that seemed to intensify the bone-deep chill he already felt.

As he grew closer, the light began to take form, solidifying into a thing sharp-edged and well-defined. Its movements ceased as though it had been waiting for him all along. A tall, freestanding mirror stood there, its impossibly smooth and flawless surface catching and distorting the surrounding light.

The mirror had no frame, no visible support, no hint of where it began or ended. It just stood there, suspended in the void, as though the fog had conjured it for his arrival.

Hugo hesitated. For a moment, nothing but the dense, white fog reflected in the mirror—a cold, damp breath on its surface—but then the glass rippled and distorted, faint images spreading out from the central point, like water disturbed by a stone.

A figure emerged, solidifying into view.

It was him—but not quite.

The reflection's hollow eyes, darker than the deepest night, stared back at Hugo, seeming to pierce through him with an icy gaze. Its sunken, sharp features showed skin stretched thin over angular bones. The mouth was tight and motionless, as if someone had carved it into place.

An involuntary shiver crawled down Hugo's spine.

The reflection moved first, its head tilting as it observed him, the movement almost serpentine. Its lips eventually parted, though the sound that followed came not from its mouth, but from the mirror itself. The voice was vacant, a hollow echo that seemed to travel vast distances before reaching his ears.

"You've been walking for a long time," it said.

Hugo hadn't expected the silence to be broken, much less by his own reflection. "I don't know where I'm going," he said in response, his voice quieter than he had intended.

The reflection's head tilted further, its expression unreadable, despite being so familiar. "You have always known," it said, sounding accusatory. "You just didn't want to admit it."

A stirring began within the surrounding fog. It moved in slow, deliberate spirals, coalescing into shapes that flickered and faded at the edges. At first, they were nothing more than vague outlines, but as Hugo watched them, they evolved into more defined shapes.

He saw a boy running through a garden, his small legs moving with a carefree energy that was unfamiliar to Hugo now. The boy's laughter was silent, but visible in the way his shoulders shook, and in how his face lit up with joy. Hugo recognised him at once.

The boy turned, his features matching those of Hugo's younger self, though they carried a lightness that had long since been extinguished. Before Hugo could call out, the boy vanished, swallowed by the swirling fog. Subsequently, he caught sight of his mother.

Frieda sat at her desk, pen in hand, her brow furrowed in concentration. She paused, her head cocked to one side as though considering her next words, then began writing again. The lines around her mouth hinted at a smile, but her eyes betrayed a deep and unspoken sadness.

A tightness gripped Hugo's chest. This scene seemed familiar, even though he'd never witnessed it. It was the moment she had written the letter he had later found after her death—the letter she had never sent.

The image blurred, then reformed. He saw Emily standing by the bench in the garden where they had met. She stood with her back to him, her wavy hair framing her shoulders. She stood motionless, as though she were waiting for something—or someone.

Hugo's heart clenched. "Emily..." He stepped towards her.

But as he reached out, the image disintegrated into the fog, scattering like windblown ash.

"You think you are the only one who has suffered?" The reflection's voice snapped Hugo's attention back to the mirror. The figure inside had moved closer, its distorted face filling more of the surface. Its tone was sharper now; every word was like a knife. "You think your pain is unique? That no one could ever understand it? Hugo, you have been dishonest with yourself—always lying. You do not covet understanding. You yearn to be exceptional."

"That's not true," Hugo said, his voice trembling. "I have wanted... I've wanted someone to see me for who I am. That is all I've ever wanted."

The reflection sneered, its lips curling into something cruel. "And yet you've hidden yourself at every turn. Behind anger. Behind indifference. Behind words that mean nothing."

Fear made Hugo take a step back, his heart thumping.

"You've been running, Hugo," said the reflection, its voice growing louder. "But not from the world. From yourself."

The fog thickened even more, the shapes within it spiralling faster, their edges smearing into total abstraction. With a violent ripple, the mirror's surface began to change, thin cracks appearing along its edges.

With an ear-splitting crack like ice breaking underfoot, the glass fractured, spreading like a spider's web. Each crack splintered the reflection into fragments, and within each shard, a different image appeared.

One reflected Emily, her bright smile dissolving into mist. Another reflected Heinrich, hunched in his chair, his hands trembling as he stared into the fire. And another reflected Hugo himself, but as a child, curled up on his bed, his small body shaking with silent sobs.

The reflection's voice swelled, a monstrous, multilayered roar, its tones clashing and grating, deeply unsettling. "What are you, Hugo?" it demanded, the weight of the words somehow causing the fog itself to tremble around him. "A man? A ghost? Or just a story you've told yourself to feel real?"

As the cracks deepened, a palpable tension filled the air, building to an unbearable crescendo; it seemed the universe itself was about to split apart.

Then the mirror shattered.

The sound was deafening, a piercing shriek that filled the void and seemed to split the air itself. Shards of glass exploded outward, but instead of falling, they disintegrated mid-flight, dissolving into the swirling fog.

Hugo staggered backward, shielding his face as the overwhelming force knocked him onto his backside.

When he dropped his arms, he saw only the suffocating, boundless white.

The fog pressed against him, dense and unyielding, until it had extinguished whatever existed of the world beyond it. Hugo remained still, his breath coming in short, quick gasps. The oppressive silence seemed to amplify his heartbeat, the rhythm loud and jarring in the void.

And then, it whispered into being.

A violin.

At first, the tune was fragile, seeming reluctant to fully emerge. Like a silver thread, the notes wound through the fog, soft and haunting. He recognised it; the same melody he had heard before, the one from the garden, the one that had once bewitched him. The melody he heard in a time when the world seemed promising to him.

His first instinct was to move, to follow the sound, to seek its source. But he remained rooted, his body unwilling—or unable—to obey his desire to rise from the ground. The music swelled, insistent and pervasive, clinging to him like the fog—a chilling yet comforting embrace. It seemed to pull at something deep within him, a place he hadn't dared touch in a long time.

The fog swirled faster as the music swelled to fill the space. It throbbed ubiquitously, its rhythm achingly familiar, composed solely for him. Hugo closed his eyes, letting the sound wash over him.

What are you?

The question surfaced again, the reflection's voice echoing in his mind. Relentless and demanding, it sliced through the violin's melody like a sharpened blade.

What are you?

The music faltered, the notes trembling like frightened birds, mirroring the tension of the question hanging in the air. Hugo's knuckles turned white as he clenched his fists, his nails digging into his palms. He wanted to answer, to scream into the void, to tear through the fog and silence the voice—to silence himself. But he could not.

Hugo woke with a gasp, his chest heaving as though he had just surfaced from drowning. The frigid air in his room bit into his damp skin, the sweat on his forehead sending a deep chill through him.

He sat up with caution, his hands gripping the edge of the

mattress to steady himself. The darkness of the room was disorienting, the shadows twisting into unrecognisable shapes. For a moment, he half-expected to see the mirror standing at the foot of his bed, its fractured surface staring back at him. But emptiness prevailed.

The violin's melody haunted his ears, dissolving into memory. He pressed his palms to his face, the coolness of his skin grounding him, though it did little to calm the storm inside.

What are you?

The reflection's last words continued to echo in the silence, a question that refused to be ignored. Hugo stared into the shadows, his mind turning over the words, trying to extract their meaning—or perhaps avoid it altogether.

Trembling fingers caught in his damp hair as Hugo ran a hand through it. The room seemed even colder now; He draped his legs over the side of the bed and sat there, staring at the outline of the window.

Though he sensed the approaching dawn, the city outside remained cloaked in darkness. The world was waking, oblivious to the question that gnawed at his very core, demanding an answer he was not sure he could give.

"What am I?"

CHAPTER THIRTY
The Prison of Time

Overnight, the snow had thinned, leaving the streets damp and slushy beneath Hugo's boots. The once-pristine white had turned to a patchwork of grey, the snowbanks lining the roads stained with soot and grime.

Once again, Hugo wandered the streets, his coat pulled tight against the wind, and his scarf flung around his neck. He had no destination, no purpose to his wandering—only a vague desire to escape the confines of his flat and lose himself in the labyrinth of stone.

He turned a corner and found himself in front of a small, unassuming shop. Mismatched items cluttered its window: dusty books, porcelain figures, tarnished silverware, and a few odd trinkets with no discernible purpose. But it was not the eclectic collection of trinkets and oddities that caught Hugo's eye. It was the clock.

It sat on a worn velvet cushion, its brass frame tarnished with age. Time itself seemed to abandon the mechanism, the hands of the clock frozen, pointing arbitrarily at 10:05.

Hugo halted, eyes locked on the clock. He did not know why it held his attention, only that he couldn't look away.

The longer he looked, the more the clock seemed to mock him. Its very existence seemed absurd—a device meant to measure the passage of time, now rendered useless by its own inability to move forward. Immobile, a single moment trapped it, rendering its purpose futile.

Time doesn't stop, he thought. *It never started. It doesn't care about where it's going. Neither do I.*

Time, to him, was always a convenient fabrication that simplified life's complexity. It was not real, not in the way people pretended it was. The ticking of a clock, the changing of seasons, the rise and fall of the sun—all of it nothing more than an illusion, a construct built to trap the mind in a linear progression.

Time, he believed, was nothing more than a cage. And he was its prisoner.

Its relentless march had dictated every moment of his life. The hours spent in the office; days spent wandering the city; years spent chasing connections that always slipped through his fingers. Time was the fictional tyrant that ruled his existence, indifferent to his desires, and indifferent to his despair.

He longed to step outside of it, to escape the confines of seconds, minutes, and hours. He wanted to experience everything all at once—the fullness of the universe laid bare before him, unbound by chronology. But that was impossible.

That's why he envied the broken clock in the window, the one that whispered, despite its hands never moving. It had broken free.

The thought should have stirred something more in him—sadness, frustration, maybe even anger—but it did not. He was long past that. The numbness that had taken root in him months ago remained unshaken, its grip as firm as ever.

He turned from the shop window and resumed his aimless walk, unaware that he was being drawn towards the sound of a church bell.

CHAPTER THIRTY-ONE
Faith

The bell tolled. Hugo did not know why it had caught his attention—he had heard many bells while living in London these past years, and this one was undistinguished. Yet, as he walked the streets, the sound pulled at him, drawing him towards its source.

The streets narrowed as he followed the fading chime, the buildings on either side growing older, their façade weathered by Father Time. The bell rang again, closer now, its note reverberating through the damp stone, settling in Hugo's chest.

As he turned the last corner, he saw the church. The building stood modest compared to London's grand cathedrals, and its steeple leaned askew. Soot and age darkened the stones, and snow gathered in uneven piles on the steps leading to its heavy wooden doors.

Hugo felt uneasy as he approached. Religion had never captured him—he never needed God, or scripture. And yet, the question that had haunted him since his dream whispered through his mind once more. *What are you?*

He pushed open the door.

He found the church interior colder than expected. A thick scent of sweet, earthy incense hung in the air, mixed with the sharp tang of old stone. The space was vast, the ceiling arching high above, supported by beams that stretched far into shadow. Only a few worn tapestries and flickering candlelight broke the bareness of the walls.

Hugo walked down the central aisle, his footsteps echoing in the stillness. The space's emptiness pressed upon him, a sentient presence observing his inaction.

But Hugo did not pray, nor did not kneel, bow his head, or clasp his hands together. He just sat in one of the pews near the middle of the room, his back straight, and his hands resting on his knees.

Silence surrounded him like a blanket, and he stayed still and unthinking for a lengthy period. He breathed, the sound of his breath echoing in the vastness of the silent church.

The emptiness of the church differed from the emptiness he carried within himself. His own void was heavy and consuming, a constant dark abyss that threatened to swallow him whole. But the church's emptiness was light, almost comforting—a space that existed not to take, but to hold.

He glanced at the altar up ahead, its surface bare save for a simple cross. Its simplicity struck him. This place lacked grandeur and ostentation. Just wood, stone, and silence.

For a moment, he envied those who believed—those who could find meaning in places like this. Those who could kneel before the altar and feel some kind of connection to something larger than themselves. But Hugo felt no connection. He felt no faith. Solace was absent.

Still, the space stirred something within him, a faint echo of an emotion he couldn't put a name to. Neither peace nor despair defined it.

Stillness.

Hugo closed his eyes, the scent of incense filling his lungs.

What are you? Again, he heard the words ringing through him, the voice from his dream as clear as if someone had spoken aloud. If he had been religious, perhaps he would have labelled it as God. His jaw tightened, and his hands clenched into fists. He didn't know the answer. He wasn't sure an answer existed.

Once more, he thought of his reflection in the mirror, the way it had sneered at him, accusing him of anger and indifference. He thought of the cracks that had spread across the mirror's surface, each one revealing a piece of his fractured life.

Hugo opened his eyes, staring at the cross on the altar. "What am I doing here?" he asked aloud to himself—to God.

He did not expect an answer, and none came.

CHAPTER THIRTY-TWO
Nothing

He had intended on heading home, but upon stepping back outside, the church door creaking shut behind him, he found himself drawn to some otherworldly call.

Patches of frost were visible on the iron fence bordering the small cemetery. The arrangement of the graves within was uneven; some markers leaned, others had cracked, and the earth had almost swallowed some. Most of the names etched into the stones were unclear, their edges softened by time and weather.

Hugo wandered between them, patches of snow crunching underfoot. He stooped to read a name: *Martha Cromwell, 1811—1887.*

He let the name settle in his mind, imagining a woman with grey hair tied in a bun, her hands calloused from years of domestic work. Perhaps she had been a seamstress, sewing by candlelight in a cramped room with a single window. Maybe she'd had children who had moved away, leaving her to grow old in solitude. Or perhaps there had been no children at all, just a tiny life that ended in a bed she had made herself.

He moved to another stone, this one simpler, its letters almost illegible. *James Tanner,* he decided it read. *1853—1862.* A child.

Hugo stared at the dates, a shiver crawling up his spine. He pictured a boy with wide, curious eyes, running through a muddy field. It's possible James spent his childhood helping his father herd sheep on the outskirts of a small village. Hugo imagined the boy coughing in the dead of winter, his breaths shallow and strained, his mother sitting beside him with unsteady hands. Somehow, the snow blanketing this grave felt heavier than the others.

Another grave caught his eye, its marker more ornate than the others around it. *Elizabeth Winters, 1835—1888.* The name struck him as poetic, almost literary. In his mind, he saw a woman who filled every space she occupied, her laughter as radiant and abundant as summer sunlight. Perhaps she had written poetry in secret, hiding it in a wooden box beneath her bed. Maybe she had known love, a fleeting but passionate affair that burned out too soon. Or maybe her life had been underwhelming—her beauty unnoticed, fading as quickly as a breath in the cold.

The graves blurred together as Hugo wandered, his mind weaving stories for each name and date he read. Some markers lacked legible names, while others only had initials or symbols, as if people forgot their occupants. He felt oddly at home among them.

The dead, he thought, were straightforward in nature. They asked for nothing, needed nothing, and gave nothing in return. Their silence soothed, devoid of expectation or judgement.

Hugo's thoughts drifted to Berlin, to his father's last words to him. *That funeral was for you both.* Walking among the graves, the words took on a different weight. Hugo considered that his father had been right; perhaps the funeral had been for him, in a way.

The sky darkened, the glow of the church's windows casting shadows over the cemetery. Hugo stopped and leaned against a tall marker with an inscription obscured by moss.

He thought of death—not just the abstract idea of it, but the finality of it. The way it erased everything, wiping clean the slate of existence.

What did it mean to die? To leave behind a world that would carry on without you, indifferent to your absence? What if it had already ceased to care about your presence?

The idea of an afterlife had always seemed absurd to him, a

comforting fiction designed to soothe the living. Heaven, hell, purgatory—they were all the same. Just illusions, crafted to give shape to the shapeless.

But nothingness—*that* he could believe in.

The thought of ceasing to exist—of dissolving into the void—was both terrifying and liberating. To no longer be bound by the confines of time; by the confines of memory; by the relentless weight of existence. What could be more peaceful than that? And yet, the idea of his thoughts, feelings, and self just vanishing into the ether registered as a betrayal of everything he had endured.

"Is it peace," he said aloud, barely audible over the sound of the wind, "or is it oblivion?"

The gravestones offered him no answers, their silence absolute.

He crouched beside another grave, brushing away the thin layer of snow that had gathered on top of it. Time had worn the name beyond recognition, reducing the letters to slight grooves in the stone. He wondered who lay beneath it.

Was it someone who had fought against death, clinging to their last moments with a sheer desperation? Or was it someone who had welcomed it, embracing the end as a release from whatever burdens they had carried?

Hugo thought of his mother. Did terror grip her in her final moments, or did she find serenity? He could not bring himself to imagine her face as she lay dying, her breaths slowing until they eventually stopped forever. No matter how hard he tried, he could not reconcile the image with the woman who had written to him. Instead, he thought of Emily.

What would she have said if she could see him now, wandering a cemetery in the dead of winter, searching for answers among the stones? Would she have laughed? Would she have called him a fool for chasing shadows? Or would she have taken his hand, led him away from the graves, and told him to stop looking for meaning where none existed?

He thought of the violin's melody, of the dream that had haunted him, and of the question that refused to leave him.

What are you?

He did not know, and he was no longer sure he wanted to.

The dead expected nothing from him, and that was perhaps why he experienced a greater sense of belonging among them than he ever had among the living. They did not ask who he was, what he wanted, or why he wandered.

Hugo's gaze rose to meet the darkening sky. He again pondered time, questioning if the dead had escaped its prison, or merely found themselves trapped in another way.

He closed his eyes, the cold nipping at this skin, and whispered into the void. "Do the dead dream of nothing?"

CHAPTER THIRTY-THREE
Letters

Stepping into the room, Hugo sensed the cold following him in the darkness. He hung his coat on the hook by the door, shaking loose the thin dusting of snow that had gathered on the shoulders. With a loosening of his scarf, he stepped into his flat.

He had performed the routine countless times, but tonight felt different. He flipped through the small stack of papers on the table near the door—a single newspaper from earlier in the week, and an unaddressed leaflet about an upcoming election were all that greeted him.

No mail.

Hugo stared at the empty space where an envelope might have been, his hand lingering on the table. He briefly, absurdly, anticipated something. He had expected a letter.

Not just any letter. Emily's letter.

His mind's eye illustrated it. A cream-coloured envelope with his name written in her neat, deliberate hand. Inside, there might be an apology full of warmth and understanding. She would explain everything—why she left, why she pushed him away, and why she hadn't written to him before.

Or maybe it would be a confession. She might admit that she, too, had been thinking of him, that leaving had been a mistake, and that she had regretted it every day since.

Perhaps it would be neither of those. Instead, maybe it would be a simple plea: *Meet me in the garden, Hugo, just as we used to. Please.*

The imagined words swirled in his mind, each scenario tugging at him differently. For a moment, the hollow ache in his chest, a constant companion for months, felt as if it might burst with a fresh emotion.

But then, as quickly as it had come, the feeling evaporated, leaving only emptiness in its wake. Hugo let out a bitter laugh, his breath visible in the chilly room. "Absurd," he said to himself, shaking his head. Emily didn't even know where he lived. The very idea was ridiculous.

He tossed the papers back onto the table and retreated to his sanctum—the small room at the back of the flat where he spent most of his evenings. A bottle of brandy waited for him on the desk, along with a glass he had neglected to clean the night before.

Hugo poured himself a generous measure before taking a seat, the chair groaning beneath him. The first sip burned his throat, but the warmth spread, dulling the edges of his thoughts.

He stared at the blank sheet of paper on the desk, the image of his mother's letter rising in his mind. He thought of her sitting at her own desk, her pen flowing across the page. She had known she could not send it—she hadn't even known where he was—but she had written it anyway, pouring her thoughts onto the page as if the act of writing could bridge the distance between them.

Hugo reached for his own pen.

Dear Emily,

He paused, the tip of his pen hovering over the paper. What could he say?

In his mind, he rehearsed telling her the truth—the painful honesty of his constant thoughts of her, the emotional toll of their last conversation still resonating within him—how he wished he could have been real in that moment… for her. He could write about the dreams, the garden, the violin, the way her departure had hollowed him out, leaving him adrift. But the words would not come.

Setting down his pen, he leaned back, swirling the brandy in his glass. The act of writing seemed futile. It seemed absurd. Emily would never read the letter.

An alternative thought struck him: he could write to his father instead.

Hugo sat upright, his mind racing. Heinrich could receive a letter—he could read the words; he could hold the paper in his hands. It would be real, it would be tangible, unlike this pointless exercise in writing to a ghost. But what would he say?

He thought of their last conversation, the confrontation that had turned the remnants of fire in his soul to ash. A vivid image of his broken, slumped father flickered in Hugo's mind, evoking a strange mix of anger and pity.

He picked up the pen again, his hand less steady than it had been before. The words refused to come.

What was the point? What could he possibly write that would change anything? His father would never understand. Even if he did, what would it matter? The past was unchangeable, a frozen lake that no amount of effort could crack. He dropped the pen on the desk.

A sudden burst of frustration overwhelmed him; he snatched the paper, its cheap texture crinkling in his grip, and ripped it in two with a sharp tearing sound. Then he tore it in half again before letting the pieces flutter to the floor like snow, scattering around his feet in uneven patches.

Silence reigned, broken only by a softly ticking clock. It mocked him. The brandy in his glass had grown warm in his hand, but Hugo didn't drink it. He sat there, staring at the torn pieces of his unwritten letter, wondering if this, too, was all he would ever be.

CHAPTER THIRTY-FOUR
A Place Outside Time

From the beginning, the garden had always been a peaceful spot, but now its silence had become uncomfortable—it pressed heavy against Hugo's soul. Patches of snow, melting under a pallid sun, lay uneven across the paths and flower beds, their damp, heavy weight smoothing the sharp edges of the world into soft, pale humps. The familiar iron gate creaked as he pushed it open, the sound swallowed at once by the garden's stillness.

Just inside, he paused, the chilly air biting at his face, his exhaled breath visible as a frosty plume. The garden had once been a place of possibility, alive with the hum of hope. Now, it seemed like a graveyard for memories, a hollow thing filled only with echoes of words he could no longer bear to recall.

Grief felt like treachery; a selfish indulgence Hugo could not bring himself to claim. Not here, not in this place once filled with so much of Emily's light. But he stepped forward anyway, the frozen path crunching in anguish as he walked over it.

The bench was just as he remembered it, though the wood looked more weathered in the frost. He lowered himself onto it, his body heavy with a weight that had nothing to do with the cold.

The garden stretched out before him; its once-vivid life subdued by more than just winter's touch. Bare branches cast faint, crooked shadows on the snow; stillness reigned, even slight movement felt disruptive.

It's strange, he thought, *how a place can hold the weight of someone's absence.*

He looked down at his hands resting limp in his lap. They were red from the cold, but he was too numb to care. This place had once been the scene of his greatest respite, a sanctuary untouched by the chaos of the city beyond its gates. Now, it felt timeless, detached from the flow of time. Or perhaps that was simply the nature of his own grief.

A sound stirred him. At first, only the faintest whisper of the violin reached him, but as he sat, the melody grew clearer, filling the air with its melancholic strains. The melody, as always, was striking yet delicate, weaving its way through the garden like a ghost. Hugo did not move.

Before, a desire to understand the captivating sounds might have tempted him to rise and find the music's source. But now, he simply sat, letting the sound wash over him.

The violin played on, its notes intertwining with the silence, filling the space with something both mournful and comforting. Hugo tilted his head back, his breath rising in thin plumes, then closed his eyes.

In an unprecedented moment, he didn't feel the need to try. The need to run, to search, to think, or to fight against the emptiness. The garden, in its muted decay, seemed to understand him in a way nothing else ever had.

Here, he was free from time, and it did not matter whether he was real.

Hugo let the melody wrap around him, the faintest smile playing at his lips—not from joy, but from acceptance. No resolution loomed, no grand epiphany awaited him in the snow-covered paths, or in the distant notes of the violin.

And that was fine.

The violin's final note hung in the air for a moment before fading into nothingness. Hugo leaned back on the bench, the cold of the wood seeping through his coat. He let out a long breath.

Snow settled around him, and for the first time, he found

IN THE ABSENCE OF SPRING

peace in knowing spring would come without him
    He didn't need it; winter had taught him how to stay.

ABOUT THE AUTHOR

Born in Scotland in 1997, Alexander Graeme has always been drawn to the unconventional—stories that twist, baffle, unsettle, and linger in the mind. A writer of many forms, he has written fantasy, literary fiction, poetry, and also short stories of various genres, weaving together introspection, surrealism, and raw emotion. His creative pursuits extend to filmmaking, where he has crafted various short films across comedy, horror, and thriller genres.

MORE FROM THIS AUTHOR

Rainier, the self-anointed 'God of Dreams' rules over the dream realm—a place where dreams from all realities take place. Rainier and those in his favour are able to harness the secrets of the dream realm to spy on their rivals, and influence their thoughts and feelings through their dreams.

Theodore, a young man living in present-day Manhattan, wakes up an unfamiliar place. At first, he believes he is dreaming, but as days pass, he begins to worry that he is actually trapped in an entirely different realm of existence.

Now stuck in the mysterious land of Utrudaf, Theo must learn to navigate the dangers of a ruthless world filled with magic, war, politics, and of course, copious amounts of wine—all to find his way home. But things are never so simply—the God of Dreams is on Theo's tail, desperate to learn how he was able to transcend realities.

Dream Farmers is an ongoing epic fantasy series from Alexander Graeme. The first two books in the series are available now, and each is told from nine alternating points of view.

Made in the USA
Las Vegas, NV
08 February 2025

a5cbef16-605d-491b-be3b-de2f85bfaaeeR03